"Could you stand in for Dad on Friday?"

Tanner didn't stand a chance. Especially when Maddie looked at him like that. Like he was her only hope.

"I'll stand in for one game, Coach. But the school will need to find a long-term replacement."

Her father's eyes drifted shut. "Th-thank…"

The nurse entered the room. "I think it's time we let your father rest."

The nurse herded them toward the elevator.

"Thank you for putting Dad's mind at ease." She slipped her arm through the crook of his elbow. "This won't be as bad as you're thinking."

He slumped. "It'll be worse."

She caught his hand. "You won't regret this, Tanner."

He already regretted this. For a multitude of reasons.

"I'll be with you every step of the way. We'll get through the game together, I promise," she said.

His heart hammered. This was *not* a good idea.

Lisa Carter and her family make their home in North Carolina. In addition to her Love Inspired novels, she writes romantic suspense. When she isn't writing, Lisa enjoys traveling to romantic locales, teaching writing workshops and researching her next exotic adventure. She has strong opinions on barbecue and ACC basketball. She loves to hear from readers. Connect with Lisa at lisacarterauthor.com.

Books by Lisa Carter

Love Inspired

K-9 Companions

Finding Her Way Back
A K-9 Christmas Reunion

Coast Guard Courtship
Coast Guard Sweetheart
Falling for the Single Dad
The Deputy's Perfect Match
The Bachelor's Unexpected Family
The Christmas Baby
Hometown Reunion
His Secret Daughter
The Twin Bargain
Stranded for the Holidays
The Christmas Bargain
A Chance for the Newcomer
A Safe Place for Christmas
Reclaiming the Rancher's Heart
A Country Christmas
Falling for Her Best Friend
Building Her a Home
The Christmas Playbook

Visit the Author Profile page at LoveInspired.com.

THE CHRISTMAS PLAYBOOK

LISA CARTER

LOVE INSPIRED
INSPIRATIONAL ROMANCE

If you purchased this book without a cover you should be aware that this book is stolen property. It was reported as "unsold and destroyed" to the publisher, and neither the author nor the publisher has received any payment for this "stripped book."

LOVE INSPIRED®
INSPIRATIONAL ROMANCE

ISBN-13: 978-1-335-23029-4

The Christmas Playbook

Copyright © 2025 by Lisa Carter

Recycling programs for this product may not exist in your area.

All rights reserved. No part of this book may be used or reproduced in any manner whatsoever without written permission.

Without limiting the author's and publisher's exclusive rights, any unauthorized use of this publication to train generative artificial intelligence (AI) technologies is expressly prohibited.

This is a work of fiction. Names, characters, places and incidents are either the product of the author's imagination or are used fictitiously. Any resemblance to actual persons, living or dead, businesses, companies, events or locales is entirely coincidental.

For questions and comments about the quality of this book, please contact us at CustomerService@Harlequin.com.

® is a trademark of Harlequin Enterprises ULC.

Love Inspired
22 Adelaide St. West, 41st Floor
Toronto, Ontario M5H 4E3, Canada
www.LoveInspired.com

HarperCollins Publishers
Macken House, 39/40 Mayor Street Upper,
Dublin 1, D01 C9W8, Ireland
www.HarperCollins.com

Printed in U.S.A.

But God commendeth his love toward us, In that, while we were yet sinners, Christ died for us.
—*Romans* 5:8

To my beautiful Riley—

In the garden of my heart, you are one of God's sweetest blossoms. I love you. Lolli

Chapter One

At 5:00 a.m., the sky was still dark when pastry chef Maddie Lovett arrived at the bakery.

Mid-September, there was just enough nip in the air to hint that crisp, autumn days would soon envelop the small mountain community of Truelove, North Carolina. Early morning had become her favorite time of the day. She loved coming in when no one else was awake yet.

Fortifying herself with a cup of coffee, Maddie took a quick moment to organize before she dived into the work orders. Dressed in her usual jeans and comfy baker shoes, she slipped the brown apron with the bakery's logo over her long-sleeved black tee. Her gaze wandered over the kitchen.

Madeline's was a dream come true. The appliances were stainless steel, commercial grade. The portable worktables on wheels maximized flexible use space. The stone-hearth oven—her pride and joy—stood fixed against the back wall.

Only a few years out of culinary school, she was grateful to local chef and mentor, Kara MacKenzie at the Mason Jar Café. Kara's investment in the little bakery had enabled Maddie's vision to come to life.

Gulping the last swallow of coffee, she glanced at the clock on the wall. Time to get to work. The display case wouldn't fill itself.

Over the next hour and a half, she baked the sourdough loaves she'd allowed to rise overnight. She inserted loaf after loaf on the long wooden paddle into the oven. A rich, grainy aroma permeated the kitchen.

Every ten minutes, the timer went off. She rotated French baguettes and cinnamon-swirl loaves in and out of the oven.

After that, she turned her attention to baking the pastries she'd preassembled the previous afternoon. Always in motion, her early-morning routine was a race against time before she opened the door to customers at 7:00 a.m.

Into the display case, she placed cranberry scones, apple turnovers, pecan sticky buns and cinnamon rolls.

Waiting on the last timer, she slipped around the counter to the front windows overlooking Main Street. Sunrise had a way of sneaking up on her. One minute it was dark, and then the next, streaks of pink and apricot filled the horizon over the smudged purple ridges of the Blue Ridge.

The town slowly stirred to life. Around the block on the other side of the square, the breakfast crowd had already started to trickle into the Mason Jar. As the sky turned golden, she unlocked the front door.

It wouldn't be long before a steady stream of customers broke the quiet calm of her morning.

The timer went off. The chocolate croissants were baked to delectable, flaky perfection. Exactly as they should be. Crouching behind the display case, she placed the mouthwatering goodness onto the tray.

When the bell above the door jangled, she rose. "Welcome to—" Her heart dropped.

Her first customer of the day stopped in their tracks. "Maddie Lovett, is that you?"

She put her hand to her throat. "Tanner?"

Those inscrutable eyes of his—like looking into the deeply layered depths of a moss-dappled brook—crinkled at the corners. "It's been a long time."

She hadn't laid eyes on Tanner Price since the day he graduated from high school and left town. But he was still as ruggedly handsome as when he'd been the star quarterback on her father's championship-winning football team.

Tanner's brow furrowed. "You've grown up."

She tilted her head. "It's been nine years since you left Truelove."

Nine years, three months and seven days, to be exact. Not that she was counting. Because that would be ridiculous.

She'd long ago moved past the hopeless, unrequited crush she'd had on the football player.

Truly. Absolutely. For sure.

Yet, feeling a flush of heat in her cheeks that had

nothing to do with the oven, she touched her hand to her head. "I'm not fifteen anymore."

His gaze followed the motion of her hand to the headband holding the masses of her unruly hair at bay. "I can see that."

She wasn't in the habit of wearing makeup to the bakery. Steam soon melted off any futile attempts at glamour. Right now, however, she deeply regretted the lack of mascara and lip gloss.

But who could have predicted the heartthrob of her youth would choose to return to Truelove today?

He studied her as if something puzzled him. "You don't wear glasses anymore?"

Tanner *would* remember those huge, owlish glasses of hers. "Contacts," she rasped.

He appeared the same—chiseled jaw, broad shoulders, knee-buckling good looks. Except his dark hair, which had once hung below his collar, was now short-cropped. He probably also had a wife and children, too.

Gathering the tattered shreds of her professionalism, she sent him the bright smile reserved for her best customers. "What can I get you?"

"I didn't realize you worked here."

She pointed to the small sign next to the old-fashioned brass register. "I own Madeline's."

"Oh." He reddened. "Maddie. I see."

"What brings you back to Truelove, Tanner?"

"I needed to check on my mom."

Maddie unwound a notch. "Is she okay?"

His manner shifted into the self-protective, aloof demeanor he'd worn like a shield during high school. "Small towns being what they are, you're probably more aware of my mother's current status than I am."

Tanner wasn't wrong. About small towns or his mother's condition.

"Small towns also care for their own."

His gaze met hers. "A person has to first want to be helped."

Like mother, like son. But that was a thought best kept to herself.

He scrubbed his hand over his stubble. "Miss GeorgeAnne promised to stay with her until I arrived."

Married, divorced or spinster, the "Miss" was an honorary title of respect bestowed on any Southern lady who was your elder. No matter if the "Miss" was elderly or not.

At fifteen, Maddie hadn't possessed the maturity to fully comprehend the bleakness of his childhood. When his father had abandoned them, his mother responded by crawling into a bottle.

But now, at twenty-four, Maddie had a better understanding of why he'd chosen to leave town. Something of her thoughts must have shown on her face.

He jutted his jaw. "I don't need your pity."

Running like a river current through his high school years, his anger had proven effective on the football field. But how well had it served him in whatever new life he'd made for himself?

She shook her head. "Sympathy is different from pity."

His eyes narrowed. "Is it?"

"Pity demoralizes." She raised her chin. "Sympathy seeks to soothe the hurt."

He looked at her a long moment before scraping his hand over his face.

"I drove all night from Florida. I haven't eaten since lunch yesterday." He grimaced. "There'll be nothing in the pantry but cigarettes and booze."

She gestured to the case. "Fresh out of the oven." As a pastry chef, her first instinct was to feed people. "What looks good to you?"

His expression unreadable, his gaze flitted to her before dropping to the case. "Definitely one of those chocolate things."

"You must be starving." She moved toward the bread case. "How about a loaf and a container of homemade chicken salad, too? The sourdough is to die for, if I do say so myself."

He gave her a slow, crooked smile. As if his wasn't a face used to smiling. "That sounds fantastic."

Reaching into the case, she removed a still-warm loaf. "I'll slice the bread for you."

He leaned against the glass. "How does a bakery come by chicken salad?"

She set the loaf into the commercial bread slicer. "Madeline's hosts an afternoon tea every fourth

Friday. I make the pastries and bread for the sandwiches. Kara from the Mason Jar supplies the fixins. Ours is a collaborative partnership."

"I'd heard someone new bought the Mason Jar."

Maddie secured the guard on the slicer and hit the button. A few seconds later, a perfectly sliced loaf of sourdough emerged.

She bagged it and handed it to him over the counter. "Paris bistro meets Southern comfort food. Kara's a renowned chef. You should stop by the Jar."

"I'm only here long enough to sort out whatever situation my mother has landed herself in this time." He broadened his shoulders. "Then I'm off to a new project."

"What kind of work do you do?"

He stuffed his hands into his jean pockets. "I maintain and repair the equipment on oil rigs."

"I'm impressed."

He shrugged. "I'm good at taking things apart and putting them together, but not much else."

She stiffened. "That's not true."

With a troubled home environment and a learning disability, Tanner had never found much success at school. But she didn't like hearing him diss himself.

"Give me one sec." She held up her index finger. "I'll get the chicken salad."

In high school, she'd peer-tutored Tanner so he could maintain his academic eligibility to play football.

She hurried toward the refrigerated cooler.

"While you're in town, I know Dad would love to reconnect with you."

"Why would Coach want to see me?"

He pursed his lips, and like a butterfly's wings, her heart fluttered against her rib cage.

"You were special to Dad." And to her.

"Coach thinks that about every team, every year."

Using a wax-paper sheet, she removed a chocolate croissant from the case. "Dad always said you had the most promise."

"A promise unfulfilled." His nostrils flared. "Always a disappointment."

She tucked several croissants into a white paper bag. "The injury you suffered at the university wasn't your fault."

"It was an injury that ended any possibility of a future football career." His mouth thinned. "Once a loser—"

She thrust the bag at him. "You are so much more, Tanner Price, than your ability to spiral a football down the length of a field."

"Yeah, well…" He scowled at the wall behind her. "Coach was the only one who believed in me."

She'd believed in him, too, but that was beside the point.

He sniffed at the air. "Is that coffee?"

"Nothing goes better with pastry than a good cup of coffee." She moved toward the fancy coffee machine at the far end of the counter. "You strike me as an Americano kind of guy."

His mouth quirked, and her knees almost buckled from the sheer gorgeousness of him.

"Am I that predictable and boring?"

Nothing about him had ever been predictable—much less boring—to her.

She placed a cardboard cup under the nozzle. "Would you trust me to select something more exotic for you?"

"Why not? You got me through my senior year, didn't you?" He gave her a genuine smile, and she nearly swooned.

Good thing he didn't smile at her more often.

"Just make sure it contains the maximum amount of caffeine possible."

She put together the concoction, capped it and handed it to him.

He took an appreciative whiff. "My flagging energy levels thank you." He reached for his wallet. "How much do I owe you for this feast?"

When she told him, he shook his head. "That seems low."

"Consider it a Welcome Home to Truelove gift from Madeline's." She threw him a shy smile. "And from me."

"You're kind." His brow furrowed. "Are you still making cookies for Coach's Thursday team-building night?"

After her mom's death, she had continued the tradition, but she was surprised he remembered. "I am."

He laid several twenty-dollar bills on the counter.

"Wait." She frowned. "That's way too much. I told you this was a gift."

"Those cookies were the highlight of my teenage life." His swift glance sent her heart thudding. "Consider this my contribution for Thursday's cookies, okay?"

Absurdly pleased he recalled her earliest baking attempts with such fondness, she gripped the edge of the counter. "Thank you, Tanner."

"Please tell your dad hi for me." He sighed. "Coach was like the father I always wanted. He's a special man. You're blessed to call him Dad."

Yes, she was.

"I don't think we'll run into each other again before I leave town, but it was good to see you, Maddie."

She swallowed past the lump lodged in her throat. "You, too, Tanner."

Then he was gone. Out of her life as quickly as he'd reappeared.

Her heart heavy in her chest, she texted her dad to let him know Tanner was in town.

Over the door, the bell jangled.

With a stream of regular customers arriving, she had no time to ponder her brief reunion with the star athlete. But all morning, an inexplicable sadness tugged at her heartstrings.

Sitting in his truck outside Madeline's, Tanner immediately dived into the pastries. He practically inhaled one of the chocolate croissants.

Based on the cookies Maddie used to bake for Coach's famous get-togethers before Friday's game, he should have guessed she'd turn out to be a baker.

Over the years, he'd thought of her—and the cookies—often. Much of his current success was due to her encouragement. He would've never been eligible to play, much less graduate from high school, if she hadn't tutored him his senior year.

So why hadn't he told her how grateful he was for her patience with him? He'd never been good with words.

As an elementary student, reading had been hard. The letters switched around in his brain. By the time he'd finally mastered reading, he was far older than the rest of his classmates. He didn't understand why he was so much dumber than his friends.

By middle school, he was overwhelmed and exhausted from never managing to complete homework that took most kids little effort. School had been a nightmare of shame. His teachers had labeled him a lost cause.

He'd longed to make his father proud, but he didn't know how. When football found him and he'd led the team to the state high school championship, though, his father was long gone.

Football was the only thing he'd ever excelled at. Until the injury during his first semester playing college ball ensured he couldn't even do that anymore.

Putting off the moment of reckoning with his

mother as long as possible, he took a closer look at his hometown.

He hadn't believed much would ever change in sleepy little Truelove, but he could see signs of change everywhere.

In a phone call to his mom a few years ago, she'd mentioned a tornado had leveled the town's iconic landmark gazebo. He peered through the oak trees lining the town square. The restored white Victorian gazebo in the middle of the town green wasn't the only thing that had changed in Truelove.

Sipping the aromatic brew from his to-go cup, he contemplated the white-washed brick and chocolate-brown awnings of Madeline's.

When he last saw Maddie Lovett, she'd been a sweet kid with overlarge glasses in various colors, matching her wardrobe. He recalled her as being fun. Quirky. Bubbly. A cute little freshman with a tangle of dark brown curls that touched her shoulders. Her eyes were like melted chocolate.

He couldn't get over how grown-up she was. How womanly.

Flushing, he cranked the engine. It had been an unspoken rule that no one messed with Coach's daughter. He would have been among the first to pulverize any dude who dared try.

He drove down Main Street toward his mom's neighborhood on the other side of the river, which wound around the town like a horseshoe.

Wave upon wave of blue-green ridges undulated across the horizon. The perpetual smoky mist, from which the Blue Ridge derived its name, called to something within him.

He was still a mountain boy at heart, but he didn't belong here anymore. Actually, he'd never felt like he belonged here.

The truck clanked over the small bridge. He barreled past the welcome sign: *Truelove—Where true love awaits.*

Not for him, it didn't.

Tanner gripped the wheel. The closer to his mother he got, the greater the tension filling him. Within a few minutes, he pulled alongside the midcentury-modern brick house where he'd grown up.

His anxiety intensified. At the front window, a curtain parted. The front door opened.

Grabbing the white bakery bag, he forced himself to get out of the truck. On the porch, his mother's long-time neighbor, GeorgeAnne Allen, embraced him in a surprising hug.

The angular, faintly terrifying woman with the short, iron-gray cap of hair was known in Truelove as the leader of the Double Name Club.

Seventysomething GeorgeAnne patted his back. "It's good to have you home, Tanner, dear."

This house had never been a home, but he let that dog lie.

"It's good to see you, too, Miss GeorgeAnne."

True to her brisk, no-nonsense nature, she soon released him. But a sheen of moisture dotted her ice-blue eyes. "It's bad this time."

The knot in his belly tightened.

"SandraLynn's spitting mad I called you, but I didn't know what else to do."

"It's okay, Miss GeorgeAnne. I'm glad you called."

They both understood it wasn't okay and never had been. Without GeorgeAnne, he'd have probably ended up like his mother—trapped in a cycle of addiction. Perhaps worse. Possibly dead or in jail.

Addiction did terrible things to people. And to the people who tried to love them.

Wherever his job took him, he called his mom once a week, but over the years he'd only returned a handful of times to Truelove. Lightning-quick visits, like a well-executed play. In and out.

The job was his excuse, but he'd also not wanted to face those like Coach, who'd believed in him so completely. People he'd failed so utterly.

He blew out a breath. "How bad is she?"

"The house is falling apart around her." GeorgeAnne's bony finger pushed her glasses higher on the bridge of her nose. "I don't think she's paid a bill in months. She's drinking more than I've ever seen. I'm not sure how she still has a job."

He raked his hand through his hair.

"I'm sorry you have to carry this, son."

He was sorry, too. It felt like he'd been sorry for his entire life. On the day his father left, the mantle of responsibility for his mother had fallen to him. And with it, the expectation to somehow fix her. To rescue her. From herself.

Yet another task at which he'd failed. In the last few months, however, he'd discovered only one thing—one person—could fix and rescue anyone.

He touched the older woman's sleeve. "Thank you for being so good to Mama."

When he'd graduated from high school, the older woman made him an unexpected deal. She'd encouraged him to accept the university scholarship to play football. In return, she'd promised to watch over his mother. And in so doing, had given him the chance for a better life.

The rough edge of GeorgeAnne's tongue caused most people to keep their distance. But during his adolescence, it was GeorgeAnne—not his unstable mother—who made sure he had something to eat every night.

Today was about fulfilling the second part of his bargain with GeorgeAnne. They'd agreed one day he would need to return to Truelove.

That day had finally come.

She lay her gnarled hand against his cheek. "You and your mama continue to be in my prayers." Her gaze skittered to the white bag he clutched. "I see you've found Madeline's. We're right proud of our Maddie." The corners of her mouth ticked up in what passed as a smile. "Some man is going to find himself mighty blessed to have her in his life."

He didn't like the sudden gleam in the older woman's eyes. The Double Name Club members were also known as the Truelove Matchmakers. A force of nature, GeorgeAnne and her matchmaking cronies were determined to help everyone in the Blue Ridge mountain town find their happily-ever-after.

Whether they wanted them to or not.

Good thing he'd escaped Truelove too young to fall into their well-intentioned crosshairs. Nonetheless, he believed it prudent to quell any unrealistic expectations his neighbor might be harboring.

"I'm sticking around only long enough to get Mama in a better headspace, Miss GeorgeAnne."

"Why, of course you are, Tanner, dear." GeorgeAnne eyed him over the top of her glasses. "Of course you are." Crossing the yard to her property, she left him alone on the porch.

Venturing inside, the house was worse than he'd feared. It would take days to restore it to some semblance of order. He riffled through the bills piled high on the mantel.

In the kitchen, he found his mother sitting in the darkness, slumped in a chair at the table. He switched on the overhead light.

"Hey!" Bleary-eyed, she lifted her head and shielded her eyes. "Turn that off."

Despite GeorgeAnne's attempt to prepare him, he was shocked at the change in her appearance.

Under the tattered blue robe, his always-slender mother was painfully thin. Her blond hair matted, the once-beautiful former homecoming queen had aged far beyond her forty-seven years. But it was her eyes he found hardest to bear. Her green eyes were glazed and full of a hopeless, helpless despair.

"Mom?"

"GeorgeAnne had no business calling you." Her mouth twisted. "I'm fine."

"You don't look fine." He swallowed. "You have a problem, Mom."

Jolting to her feet, she swayed. "I *don't* have a problem." He reached out to her, but she batted his hand away. "Despite what you think, I'm not an alcoholic." She lifted her chin. "Alcoholics drink every day. I only drink on the weekends to relax."

"It's Tuesday." He gritted his teeth. "And it's obvious you're more than worse for wear."

Dropping her gaze, she leaned heavily upon the table. "I had a bad day yesterday. It was the anniversary of the divorce."

"You should talk to someone, Mama."

She should have talked to someone fifteen years ago about her depression, but despite repeated urgings from her friends, she would never swallow her pride enough to seek professional counseling.

"Everybody has an off day now and again."

His frustration mounted. She'd been having an "off day" for years.

"I just need to get some rest."

As he helped her sit, his nose wrinkled. She stank of liquor and cigarettes.

"I'll be right as rain after a good night's sleep. You'll see." After waving him off, she folded her arms on the table. "Just need to rest."

"When was the last time you ate, Mom?"

Her eyelids drooped, and she laid her head on her arms. "Don't know…" she mumbled.

"Don't go to sleep yet." He gently roused her. "Not until you eat something."

GeorgeAnne had left a pot of coffee brewing. He quickly put together a chicken salad sandwich for his mother.

He placed both in front of her. "Maddie Lovett sent this over for you."

"Always such a sweetheart, that girl." His mother took a few birdlike bites. "Sweet on you." She pushed away from the table. "I want to lay down."

First, he made her wash her face and brush her teeth. Then he walked her to her bedroom. Easing her into the bed, he tucked the covers around her.

His mother patted his cheek. "You're a good son, Tan-Tan."

Tears stung his eyelids. He blinked them away. She hadn't called him that in a long time.

"Just need to sleep…" she whispered.

More like sleep it off.

He shut the door behind him and sagged against the wall. The all-too familiar, toxic cocktail of fatigue, guilt and anger churned in his belly.

Closing his eyes, he prayed to reclaim the peace he'd only recently found. "Help her, Father," he rasped. "Help me."

Over the next couple of hours, he hunted down and disposed of as many bottles of alcohol as he could find. But, with a sinking heart, he realized helping his mother get her life on track was going to take longer than he'd anticipated.

He had vacation days accrued. He could postpone reporting to the new project for a few weeks. He hoped he wouldn't lose his job over this.

A knock sounded. After scraping his chair out from the table, he threw open the back door.

"Coach Lovett." His heart leaped inside his chest. "What are you doing here?"

The burly fiftysomething man's face creased into a smile. "I'm here for you, son." Coach's meaty hand clamped on to his shoulder. "I'm here for you."

An unexpected answer to his prayer. Gratitude filled his heart. For the first time in a long time, Tanner didn't feel so alone.

Chapter Two

"I come bearing lunch." Standing on the back porch, Coach Lovett held up a takeout box from the Mason Jar. "There's enough for SandraLynn, too."

"Thank you, Coach." Tanner ushered Maddie's father into the kitchen. "Mom will probably sleep the rest of the afternoon, but I'll save some for her to eat later."

Coach set the bag on the oval table.

"Please excuse the mess." Shoving aside the paperwork he'd been attempting to organize, Tanner cringed, thinking what the place must look like to Maddie's dad. "Mom hasn't been feeling well."

It was a polite fiction—code for his mother had been drinking—he knew Coach would understand. The same flimsy excuse he used throughout high school for why his mom was the only mother never able to make a single game.

Although, he had preferred she not attend, rather than embarrass both of them while she stumbled around three sheets to the wind.

He gestured for Coach to take a seat. "Shouldn't you be teaching?"

Coach sank into the ladder-back chair. "Teacher workday."

Don Lovett wasn't only the football coach. He was also the school athletic director and taught ninth-grade Civics, too.

"Croque monsieur. That's grilled ham and cheese to country bumpkins like you and me." Coach shoved one of the takeout boxes across to Tanner. "One bite, and you'll thank me."

For a few moments, they ate in companionable silence. Tanner asked how the team was shaping up this year. Coach gave him the rundown on their progress since practice began in July. "First game was third Friday in August."

Coach rubbed his chest just then.

Tanner frowned. "Are you okay?"

"Just a touch of indigestion." Coach straightened. "Maddie gets on me about eating too fast."

Pushing his concerns aside, Tanner finished his sandwich.

Coach beamed at him. "It's been too long. I missed you, son."

"I couldn't face Truelove after I let everyone down." Tanner dropped his gaze. "After I let *you* down."

"You didn't let anyone down." Coach's face clouded. "Certainly not me."

Tanner sighed. "All the special training you gave me. The plans for a future in the NFL."

"Sometimes God has other plans for us. Plans we don't always—"

Tanner gave him a look.

Coach chuckled. "Okay, plans we don't usually understand, at least at first. But we trust His plans for us will be better than anything we could have imagined for ourselves."

Tanner now appreciated how many small nuggets of faith Coach had dropped into his life over the course of his high school career. Preparing the soil of his heart for the day he was able to ask his own questions about faith.

A bead of sweat broke out on the coach's forehead. "Everything has a way of working out in the end." Maddie's father wiped his brow with his hand.

Tanner sent a pointed look in the direction of his mother's bedroom. "Since when?"

Coach tugged at his golf shirt collar. "It's been my experience that if it's not okay, then it's not the end. Trust Him. Easier said than done, I know."

Tanner stood up. "Can I get you another bottle of water?"

Coach seemed unable to catch his breath. "That—that would be great."

Tanner grabbed a water bottle from the fridge.

Coach unscrewed the cap and then took a long swig. "Thanks. That's better."

"Are you sure you're okay?"

"I rushed around this morning. Got overheated. After practice this afternoon, it's Parent-Teacher Night. It's going to be a long day."

"You shouldn't have bothered with me."

Coach shook his head. "Son, you're the highlight of my busy day. An old codger like me is bound to have the occasional twinge."

Tanner leaned forward. "You've been having pain? Where? In your chest? Shouldn't you see a doctor?"

"You sound like Maddie. A doctor won't tell me anything I don't already know." He patted his stomach. "I could stand to lose a few pounds and get more exercise. But I do love my spicy tacos."

Tanner cleared the table of the remains of their lunch.

Coach cocked his head. "After your injury, did the university rescind the athletic scholarship?"

"They did."

Coach's mouth flattened. "I was afraid of that."

Tanner shrugged. "Getting diagnosed with dyslexia right before high school graduation made me eligible for other scholarships designed for students with learning disabilities. The college counselor set me up with test-taking accommodations, smaller classes and peer tutors."

Coach smiled. "Like Maddie." It had been his idea for his daughter to tutor Tanner.

Her father didn't know the half of it, though. Maddie had been the one to push him, despite his vehement teenage opposition, to seek answers for why he struggled so much at school.

"I was blown away when I stopped by Madeline's this morning."

Coach crossed his arms over his barrel chest.

"It's quite the place, isn't it? She's done well. Her mom would be so proud. I sure am."

Maddie had lost her mom a few months before Tanner made the team as a freshman. One of the things they had in common—losing a parent. She'd been about the same age as Tanner when his father had deserted him and his mother.

Coach's kind blue eyes surveyed him. "I want to hear about what you've been doing since you left Truelove."

From the photos at Coach's house during the Thursday pregame dinners, he'd gathered Maddie was very like her petite dark-haired, dark-eyed mother.

Not that he needed to be thinking about Maddie's eyes. *So* not appropriate with Coach's daughter.

He fidgeted. "I got into mechanics."

"Automotives?"

"The petroleum industry."

"Oil rigs?" Coach rested his hands on either side of the takeout box. "Sounds dangerous."

"My job takes me all over the world."

"Do you love the work?"

"I don't hate it, but a typical hitch—tour of duty on the rig—can last anywhere from twenty-eight days offshore to several months, depending on the issue. With my mom's situation..." His gaze flicked to the hallway. "It's something I may need to rethink."

"Sounds isolating and lonely."

It was, although, until this moment, he hadn't stopped long enough to acknowledge it.

Checking his phone, Coach rose. "I better get back to the office." Tanner got out of his chair, too.

"When Maddie told me you were home, there was another reason I wanted to see you. To ask for a favor." Coach appeared uncharacteristically hesitant. "Would you stop by practice this afternoon?"

Tanner's stomach lurched. He hadn't been on a football field since the game that ended his college career. "Coach..."

Maddie's father shot a quick look at Tanner and dropped his gaze again. "My current quarterback could use a few pointers from the guy with a golden arm, who's been where he is and then some."

Tanner frowned. "*Former* golden arm."

Coach pinched his broad forehead. "Friday's game is against Marshall."

Tanner gave a low whistle. "Those guys have always been tough."

"Four games into the season, we're undefeated, so of course I want us to win the game. But I also don't want my boys to get hurt in the process."

Ever since Tanner's days on the playing field, their district rival had a notorious reputation for roughing the passer, and the kicker, and any other player in their vicinity.

Coach paused at the back door. "I'd appreciate your input, but I understand if you don't feel able to leave your mom."

In the soft glow of the afternoon sun, Tanner

realized that in the years since they'd last met, Coach's hairline had continued to recede and new lines creased his craggy features. How could he refuse the man who'd stood in the gap for him when no one else would?

He rubbed his chin. "Practice still at two forty-five?"

"And done by five." Maddie's father went into coach mode. "We focus on defense the first half of practice. Offense next. Then we work with the special teams for the remainder of the time."

The split practice was the same as in Tanner's day. Don Lovett was a championship-winning coach. If it wasn't broke, no need to fix it.

Maddie's father examined his face. "But what about SandraLynn?"

To thwart their archrival, GeorgeAnne—a rabid Truelove High football fan—would probably be glad to check on his mother. He'd only be gone a few hours.

"I think it's doable." Tanner extended his hand. "I owe you so much."

Coach squeezed his hand. "You owe me nothing. You're one of the finest young men I ever had the joy to coach."

Tanner promised to meet him in the locker room in a few hours. Then he tackled the worst of the mess in the kitchen.

Strangely enough, the prospect of being out on the field again ignited something inside him he'd believed forever dead. For the first time in a long while, the idea of a pigskin in his hands sparked anticipation and not dread.

Loading the dishwasher, he reflected on the turn the day had taken. All because he'd stopped at a bakery and run into Maddie, who'd put his reunion with Coach in motion.

Perhaps Coach was right. Things might just work out. For all of them.

Maddie didn't get a chance to talk with her dad about whether he'd managed to connect with Tanner Price.

By the time the bakery closed Tuesday afternoon and she'd finished prepping dough for the next day, her dad was at practice. Since it was Parent-Teacher Night, he didn't bother coming home for dinner. Of necessity an early riser, she was already in bed asleep when he returned later that evening.

Wednesday morning was a rinse and repeat of the previous day. At precisely 7:00 a.m., she unlocked the front door. Her first customer was waiting outside Madeline's on the sidewalk.

It was Tanner. Stepping aside, she waved him into the bakery.

She touched her hand to her headband. "Hi." She bit off a sigh.

No mascara or lip gloss today, either. She really needed to rethink her early-morning beauty routine—at least until Tanner left town.

He pointed at her head. "Is that flour in your hair?"

"Oh." Blushing, she wiped her hands on her apron and swiped at the hair at her temple. "Better?"

"You're good." His eyes crinkled. "Surprised to see me again?"

More like delighted. But she'd never say that out loud. Trying not to be as big a dork as he remembered, she feigned a nonchalance she was far from feeling.

"I wasn't sure you were still in town. It's nice to see you again."

And it was. So great. Really great.

She slipped behind the counter, putting the patisserie case between them. For the sake of her rapidly thumping heart.

"It's going to take a few days longer than I planned to take care of my mom."

Maddie clasped her hands under her chin. "Is she okay?"

"As okay as it gets for her these days." He gave her a tentative smile. "The bread and chicken salad were amazing." Then Tanner glanced away. "She's better this morning and headed to work."

He meant she was sober this morning. During the year she'd peer-tutored him, he often employed euphemisms to protect his mother's pride and his own.

"I'm happy to hear that, Tanner."

He cleared his throat. "Thanks for letting your dad know I was in town."

She knotted her hands in her apron. "I wasn't

sure if you'd be mad, but Dad cares so much about you I knew he'd want to see you."

Tanner scanned the display case she'd filled with fresh-baked pastries. "He brought lunch and convinced me to assist him at practice yesterday afternoon."

"Like you don't have enough to deal with." She made a face. "Dad gets so laser-focused on football. I'm sorry."

His gaze snapped to hers. "I'm not." A small smile curved his lips. "It was fun. Meeting the team. Getting back into the action, even if from the other side of the bench."

"I'm sure he's grateful. In rural districts like Truelove, there's never enough money to hire an assistant coach."

Tanner nodded. "I remember."

"I—I didn't expect to see you again." Feeling shy, she fell back on what she knew best—pastry. "Is there something I can get you this morning?"

He dragged his eyes from the pastry to hers. "I didn't expect to be here, but turns out I find Madeline's impossible to resist."

She smiled. "What would you like?"

"You." He flushed. "I mean, why don't you pick for me?"

She willed herself to not react to the slip of his tongue. "What about the chocolate croissant? Maybe one of those again?"

"Definitely." He studied the glass case. "Every day should start with chocolate."

"I agree, but you could also sample a cinnamon bun. It's Dad's personal fave."

"When in Truelove, why not one of each?" Glancing up at her, he grinned. "There are no pastry shops on an oil rig."

"If only all my customers were as easy to please as you." She reached for a square of wax paper. "To go, like yesterday?"

"Not to go."

He rubbed the back of his neck. A gesture she recalled he did when he was feeling unsure of himself. Like before an exam or when confronted with writing an essay.

"I thought I might stick around awhile, answer work messages and catch up with you." His Adam's apple bobbed in his tanned, corded throat. "If you're not too busy. Between customers."

Something warm, like butter melting down the sides of a perfectly baked biscuit, traveled from her head to the soles of her feet.

Tanner Price wanted to spend time with her?

Ridiculously flattered, she made a real effort not to geek out on him. "Sure. Why not? Of course."

He surveyed her cozy little realm. "Maybe you could join me with one of those fabulous coffees. If you don't mind me claiming one of your tables."

A sudden giddiness seized her. "That's what the tables are there for, right? For people to claim."

Stop talking. Just stop talking.

For several seconds, she busied herself with

plating the pastries. "I'll bring it over to you," she mumbled.

The next few minutes were like her teenage dreams come true. Not that she would have ever had the courage to dream about a real conversation that didn't involve Senior English Lit and *Wuthering Heights*, of course.

But that's exactly what happened. She and Tanner Price talked about their lives.

"You've lived in some exciting places." She warmed her hands around her coffee mug. "Texas. Alaska. New Orleans."

"Most of the time, I lived on the oil rig." He took a sip of coffee. "I only occasionally visited those places when I had shore leave."

He wanted to know how she'd ended up owning Madeline's. "So, are you a pastry chef or a baker?"

Taking a bite of the cinnamon bun, he practically moaned with pleasure. For her, it was the highest compliment.

"At college, I specialized in the pastry arts. So I'm a pastry chef. But because Madeline's is in a small town, I bake lots of different desserts to appeal to as many people as possible." She tucked a tendril of hair behind her ear. "As long as people call me for their next sweet-treat order, either works."

His smile faded. "There's actually something I've wanted to say to you for a long time, Maddie." His gaze locked on hers. "But it's always been hard for me to express my feelings."

Feelings? For her? Her heart did a somersault. What did he mean?

He cleared his throat. "Maddie, I—"

The front door flew open. The bell clanged wildly. Her father stumbled inside. She and Tanner jumped to their feet.

Maddie reached for him. "Dad, are you feeling okay?" His hand felt clammy.

Her father rubbed his chest. "Not feeling in tiptop shape this morning, but I'm sure it'll pass."

Tanner frowned. "Maybe you should get checked out at the ER. You weren't feeling good yesterday, either."

"Why am I only now hearing about this?" She shot Tanner and her father an irritated look. "You aren't taking care of yourself, Dad."

"I'm feeling sick to my stomach, but I'm still getting over my cold from last week." Her father waved away her words. "I just need to lie down for a bit. Maybe I'll take the day off from school before practice this afternoon."

She scowled. "Why is it that all you ever think about is that stupid leather ball?"

Her father snorted. "'Cause I'm the football coach?"

"Your symptoms seem more serious than the aftereffects of an upper-respiratory infection, Dad."

"I'd be happy to drive you to your doctor, Coach."

Her father rolled his eyes. "You two are making a mountain out of a molehill. I tell you I'm—"

Suddenly, he clutched his left arm. His complexion went ashen. Staggering, he then collapsed into a heap on the floor.

"Dad!" she screamed. "Tanner, what's happening to him?"

Tanner dropped to his knees. "He's having a heart attack."

"Help him, Tanner. Please help him." Crouching beside her listless father, she took his hand. "Dad! Can you hear me? Answer me, Dad."

Tanner immediately began performing CPR on her dad.

Willing her father to fight hard to stay alive, she held on to his hand. "What can I do, Tanner? How can I help him?"

"Five…six…seven…" Tanner counted off the chest compressions. "Call 911," he rasped.

She fumbled for the cell phone in her pocket. When she reached the operator, she barely recognized the reedy, thin, panicked sound of her own voice.

"They're on their way."

Pinching her dad's nostrils closed, Tanner gave her father two quick puffs of breath.

Tears cascaded down her face. "Stay with us, Dad. Don't leave me."

A siren went off across the square. The fire department was only around the block. However, the closest ER was on the other side of the mountain. Her gut clenched. Would the paramedics be able to get him there in time?

Please, God. Save my dad. Don't let him die.

Gripping his hand, she pressed her face against his knuckles. "I love you, Dad. I love you so much. Please don't die."

The ambulance squealed to a stop outside, and the paramedics barreled through the door.

One of the EMTs moved her aside to get to her father. She scrambled to her feet. The other paramedic took over the chest compressions from Tanner.

His hands on his thighs, Tanner leaned against the cake-display counter.

The first EMT did a rapid assessment. "Prepare for defibrillation." He switched on the device and ripped open her father's dress shirt. Buttons pinged across the floor.

The EMT attached pads to his chest. "Clear," he called.

Stopping the chest compressions, the other paramedic took his hands off her father.

At the sudden surge of electricity, her father's body arched. Crying out, she put her hand over her mouth.

The paramedic checked for a pulse. He shook his head. "Again."

Her knees buckled, but Tanner caught her in his arms.

The EMT shocked her father once more, but this time, his partner nodded. "Got a pulse."

She sagged. *Thank You, God. Thank You.*

"Ready for transport." The EMT put away the defibrillator. "I'll notify the hospital we're enroute."

The paramedics strapped her dad onto the foldable stretcher.

"We're headed to Regional," the older of the two EMTs informed her.

"I—I have to close the shop, but I'll be right behind you."

Tanner shook his head. "I'll drive. You just make sure the ovens are switched off."

She was quivering like a beech leaf in a winter squall. If it hadn't been for Tanner's support, she wasn't sure she could have remained upright.

The paramedics wheeled her dad into the waiting ambulance.

Siren blaring, the ambulance sped away. Wringing her hands, she did a slow 360. Maddie burst into tears.

Tanner lifted her chin with the tip of his index finger. "Just show me what to do. I'll help you shut the bakery down, and we'll be on our way."

"I'm scared, Tanner," she whispered. "What if—"

"No *what if*s." He wrapped his arms around her. "I'm not leaving you to face this alone, Maddie."

Closing her eyes against the fear, she laid her head in the hollow of his shoulder.

"We'll get through this with Coach, together. I promise," he whispered into her hair.

She took comfort in the solid strength of him. And she prayed as she'd never prayed before that God wouldn't allow her father to die.

Chapter Three

Tanner shepherded Maddie through the sliding glass doors into the emergency room. The pungent smell of antiseptic assaulted his nostrils. They hurried to the reception desk.

"My father..." she rasped. "Donald Lovett... Is he... Has he..." Placing her hand on her chest, she struggled to breathe.

The sixtysomething receptionist rose. "Are you all right?"

He turned toward Maddie. "She's hyperventilating."

Alarm etched itself across the older woman's features. "Should I call someone?"

"Give us a minute first." He touched Maddie's shoulder. "Slow, even breaths. In through your nose for five counts. Out through your lips."

His hand resting lightly on her, he continued counting for her until the panic left her eyes and she was able to regulate her breathing.

"I'm sorry." She gripped the edge of the reception desk. "That's never happened to me before."

"A normal reaction to extreme stress and anxiety." He drew her into the protective circle of his arm. "Are you okay?"

She nodded. "What about my father?"

The receptionist typed on her computer's keyboard. "Donald Lovett's being assessed by the cardiac surgeon on call in the ER. They're running tests."

Her gaze softened at Maddie's obvious distress. "Why don't you wait for Dr. Singh in waiting room three?" She motioned toward the double doors at the end of the hall. "I'll buzz you and your husband through."

Blushing, Maddie stiffened. "He's not—"

"Thank you so much..." Taking hold of Maddie's arm, he peered at the woman's name tag. "Mrs. Puryear."

The receptionist pressed a button on the desk. "What a lovely couple you two make."

"But—but..." Maddie sputtered.

He towed her toward the slowly opening double doors. "Let's not look a gift horse in the mouth, *darling*." He gave a final wave to their benefactress as the doors swung shut behind them.

"Why did you let her believe we were together?"

He hustled her down the white-tiled corridor. "We are together, Mads."

"Not *together*-together." Maddie threw out her hands. "She thought I was your wife."

He steered her into the empty waiting room. "Hospitals have differing visitor policies. I didn't want to take the chance she might not let me through since I'm not family." He frowned. "Would you prefer I leave?"

"No." She snagged hold of his shirtsleeve. "I'm so glad you're here with me."

A doctor in blue scrubs entered the waiting room.

Dr. Singh introduced himself. "Your father has suffered a myocardial infarction. Tests reveal this was caused by coronary artery disease. It's when the arteries that supply blood to the heart narrow or become blocked."

She gulped. "What can be done for him?"

"We're prepping him for emergency surgery right now."

She wrapped her arms around herself. "Ohhhh…"

"There are major blockages in two arteries. He will need to undergo bypass surgery to allow the blood to travel more freely through his body."

Tanner pulled her closer. "How risky is this procedure?"

"It's a major surgery, but barring further complications, I am confident your father will have a good outcome." The doctor rubbed his chin. "I'll return with an update once he's post-op, but the surgery may take up to six hours."

She blinked away tears. "Thank you for everything you're doing for my dad, Dr. Singh."

The doctor left them, and Tanner guided her to the couch. "I know your dad is uppermost on your mind." He sank down beside her. "But are there people who should be notified about what's happening?"

"Definitely the school principal, Ms. Moore. Someone will have to cover Dad's classes, and football practice will need to be canceled."

He squeezed her hand. "I'll contact the school and explain everything."

"Don't you need to get back to your mom?"

"I'll ask GeorgeAnne to look in on her, but Mom should be at work until this evening anyway."

Still wearing her Madeline's apron, Maddie knotted her hands in her lap. "Please ask Miss GeorgeAnne to alert the prayer chain."

"Anyone else I should contact?"

"Kara." Her lower lip trembled. "I'm not sure when I'll be able to reopen, but I hate for the bread and pastries to go to waste. Maybe she can use them at the Jar."

After getting the numbers from her, he made the calls. GeorgeAnne promised to activate the prayer group and look out for his mother.

"But if you'd rather not stay at the hospital, Tanner, I can arrange for someone to sit with Maddie."

He frowned into the phone. "I don't mind staying with her, Miss GeorgeAnne." No way was he leaving Maddie.

"If you're sure..."

There was nowhere else he wanted to be. "I'm sure."

For a skittish arm's-length-relationship guy like him, it was a surprising revelation.

"I see." GeorgeAnne fell silent for a beat. "Well, then."

Well, what? He didn't want GeorgeAnne to get the wrong idea about him and Maddie. When it came to the matchmakers, it was never a good idea to put a target on your back.

"We're friends, Miss GeorgeAnne," he growled. "That's all. Friends help friends."

"Of course, dear heart. Absolutely."

A thread of amusement ran through her voice—always a serious red flag with a matchmaker. Their amusement often came at a cost for the recipients of their matrimonial endeavors.

But the only important thing was helping Maddie get through this day. He'd straighten out GeorgeAnne and deal with the fallout later.

He promised to keep the Double Name Club leader updated.

A long, frightening morning turned into a long, anxious afternoon. Maddie's friend Chloe stopped by to offer her support. Her fiancé, Noah Brenden, looked vaguely familiar.

Tanner could have gone all day without human contact, but for never-met-a-stranger Maddie, their visit buoyed her spirits.

"Chloe Randolph, right?" Seated next to Maddie, he tried to recall specifics. "You were a year ahead of me in high school."

The petite brunette smiled. "That's right."

"Chloe is a music therapist." Maddie turned toward the dark-haired man in the adjoining chair. "Noah is a preservation carpenter. He rebuilt the gazebo and helped complete the renovations on the old Lyric movie theater last spring."

Still trying to place where he'd seen the carpenter before, Tanner shook his hand. "Nice to meet you."

"Likewise." Noah reached for Chloe's arm. "Maddie's doing our wedding cake."

From the look they exchanged, it was obvious they were in love. A twinge of something akin to envy skittered through his heart. Weird, since he usually preferred his solitary existence to romantic entanglements.

He glanced at Maddie. "I didn't realize you did cakes, too."

"Madeline's Special Occasion Cakes are a side gig." She turned to the bubbly music therapist. "We need to schedule a cake tasting soon so you and Noah can finalize your choices."

"The sooner, the better." Noah grinned. "I'm all about cake tasting."

"Me, too." Tanner laughed. "Unless it's only for people getting married."

Her cheeks coloring to a soft pink, Maddie folded her hands in her lap. "A special occasion can be any occasion. Not only weddings."

"I might have to order a cake for myself, then." He cocked his head, trying to place Noah. "Brenden, is it? Your face sure seems familiar."

Noah chuckled. "Try Knightley."

Tanner's mouth fell open. "Oh, wow. Of course. *The* Noah Knightley." He gaped at him. "No offense, but how did a famous country singer become a carpenter living in Truelove, North Carolina?"

"Best career choice I ever made." Noah smiled. "Meet me at the Jar for lunch one day, and I'll tell you how reconnecting with Chloe changed my life forever."

"I'd like that, but I'm only in town for a few days to help my mother. Then I'm headed to a new project on the North Sea."

Maddie reared a fraction. "The North Sea?"

Chloe's eyes widened. "What do you do?"

"I'm a maintenance engineer on oil rigs."

Noah's brows raised. "That's rugged work. I'm impressed."

Maddie smiled at her friends. "Tanner's always been smart with mechanical things."

In the South, being called smart could be a compliment to a person's intelligence or an indication the person was a hard worker.

He reckoned the latter applied to him. He was no great shakes in the academic department. But he suspected Maddie meant it both ways.

She'd believed in him from the beginning. It made him want to be the man he saw reflected in her eyes.

Noah offered to transport her car from the alley behind the bakery to her house. Soon after they left, her pastor, Reverend Bryant, arrived with food sent by Kara MacKenzie at the Jar.

"Kara said not to worry about anything. She placed a notification in the window at Madeline's that the bakery would be closed due to a family emergency."

The tall, thin man with the gentle scholarly face seemed kind. "Is there anything I can do for you or your father, Maddie?"

"Dad needs your prayers." She swallowed. "So do I."

"You can count on that." He squeezed her hands. "And on the prayers of the rest of Truelove, too."

After praying with them, he promised to check on them later.

Maddie didn't have much appetite—neither did Tanner—but he insisted she try to eat something. "It'll do Coach no good if you're faint from hunger. You've got to keep up your strength. He would also remind you to keep the faith."

Sighing, she reached for the pimento cheese–stuffed French baguette. "I never heard you mention faith before."

Her dark eyes went large. "Not that we were like best friends. Not like we were anything." She fluttered her hands. "You were a senior..."

In the emotionally fraught world of high school, the senior-freshman barrier was a social apartheid all its own. Of course, they were no longer in high school.

With an endearing nervous gesture, she touched the headband keeping the dark, curly waves of hair out of her face.

He fisted his hands, half afraid he would give in to the urge to satisfy his curiosity.

"The whole prayer-faith thing is a recent development for me." He raised his eyebrow. "Faith was never part of the equation with my family. If it had been, I suspect many things would've turned out differently. Not only for me but for my mother, too."

"Recently, you say?" Dropping her gaze, she fiddled with her sandwich. "I'm sorry. It's none of my business. I know you value your privacy."

But he found himself longing to talk through with her the things he was still trying to wrap his mind around.

"Last year, on a job in Houston, there was this guy, a real family man... Reminded me of Coach. He helped me understand there was a Father who would never leave me like my father did."

She touched his arm. "I'm glad."

"Me, too. It's been..." He took a quick breath. "Life-changing. Transformative."

Then he got a little lost in the melted chocolate puddles of her eyes.

His heart pounding, he jerked his gaze somewhere safer. And concentrated on regulating his suddenly accelerated breathing.

He straightened. "Reverend Bryant seems like a down-to-earth pastor. If I wasn't leaving soon—"

"Must you? Leave soon, I mean."

He hunched his shoulders. "Other than football, Truelove doesn't have many great memories for me. Once I get Mom on the right track, I have a job waiting."

"Perhaps you could make new memories in Truelove. Happier ones."

He shook his head. "I'm not one for sticking around."

Just as well he was moving on. Sweet, innocent Maddie. There was something about her that appealed to the boy he'd once been. Before his dad had walked out and his mom had fallen to pieces. The boy who'd wanted to be somebody's hero.

But after a lifetime of failing to help his mother, he'd realized he'd never be anybody's hero.

Maddie deserved somebody far better. Someone who wasn't damaged like him.

One day, she'd find a hero worthy of her. His stomach twisted. But it wouldn't—couldn't—be him.

"It's kind of you to sit with me while we wait for Dr. Singh." She dropped her gaze. "I'll be okay if you need to go to your mom."

Was she giving him permission to leave? Giving him an out?

Normally, he would have seized any chance to avoid emotional involvement, but stubbornness rose within him. Suppose he didn't want to leave her at the hospital by herself? Suppose he didn't want to walk away from her?

Which was insane because he ought to be putting as much distance between them as possible.

For her sake.

Her hair—that glorious hair—fell forward over

her face. He hated not being able to see her expressive eyes.

Tanner set his jaw. "I'm staying with you until Coach is out of the woods."

"But—"

"Look. We might not have been best pals, Maddie. But we were friends. You saved my life."

Her eyes narrowed. "What are you talking about?"

"It was you who showed me that if I listened to the audio version of those English lit books, I could comprehend the contents as well as anyone. That I wasn't as stupid as my dad said I was."

Maddie's eyes rounded. "He *never* said that to you."

"He did." Tanner snorted. "All the time. He called me a stupid, lazy, good-for-nothing son."

"That's so not true," she sputtered.

Her outrage on his behalf for the long-ago emotional wounds caused by his father assuaged a hurt in his heart he hadn't realized was still there.

"You figured out how to incorporate the color coding I used for plays on the football field into studying for tests. It was you who insisted—against my objections—I see the guidance counselor for testing."

She bit back a small smile. "Dad says I'm bossy. But in my defense, you weren't the easiest kid to tutor."

He hadn't thought of himself as a kid in a long time. Not since his dad had walked out and his childhood ended. But she had a way of bringing out the kid in him.

"Seriously, Mads, you changed my life. You can't imagine the relief it was to know I wasn't as dumb as everybody believed."

Maddie went rigid. "You were never dumb. You merely needed a different way to accomplish the tasks."

He leaned forward, his elbows on his knees. "You gave me the greatest gift anyone could have given me—hope for a future. Thank you."

She blinked at him. "I had no idea."

"I know you didn't. But I've always wanted to thank you. And now I have."

"That's what you wanted to tell me before Dad came into the bakery?"

He nodded.

"It really was my pleasure to help you, Tanner."

He didn't doubt it. Because that was the kind of person she was. Like Coach. And he was grateful for the gift God had given him by placing them in his life. His gaze found hers.

They looked at each other for a long, long moment.

When Dr. Singh returned to the waiting room, Maddie surged to her feet.

"Good news." The heart surgeon smiled. "The operation was successful. Your father is in the cardiac intensive care unit."

Rising, Tanner entwined his fingers through hers. "ICU?"

"Standard procedure. He'll remain there today so we can monitor him. But if he continues to improve—and I am optimistic he will—he'll transfer out of CICU tomorrow. However, he'll need to remain in the hospital at least five days."

She clasped her hands under her chin. "Thank you for helping my dad, Dr. Singh."

"I'm recommending he go to a long-term rehab center for another month. His care will transfer to Dr. Martin, a highly respected cardiologist. Dr. Martin will oversee your father's postoperative care."

The doctor shot a glance at the clock on the wall. "Your father should be coming out of anesthesia soon. If you and your—your..." He tilted his head.

"Friend," Tanner supplied. "Her very good friend."

The doctor smiled. "Give the nurses time to make him comfortable, but I think you and your *very good friend* can visit him in about an hour. I'm sure your father is anxious to see you."

She spent the next hour texting friends, including her business partner, Kara, with the latest update. A male nurse took them upstairs to the CICU. As soon as they entered the unit, Maddie started shaking.

It was extremely cold in CICU, more so than the rest of the hospital. But it wasn't only the temperature.

Patients were hooked up to a myriad of machines. Monitors beeped. The CICU was intimidating. Tanner put his arm around her shoulders.

The nurse escorted them to a small room on the right side of the central hub of the nursing station. "His voice will be sore since we've removed the breathing tube. Try not to overtax him. Please limit your visit to ten minutes. After he's had a chance to rest, you can visit him again in a few hours."

Lying on the hospital bed, Coach was pale, but he turned his head toward them. "M-Maddie..."

She rushed forward and gripped his hand. "It's so good to see you, Dad." Tears rolled down her cheeks.

Coach's eyes were not as bright as usual, but he was alert. "Tannn..." He lifted his other hand.

"I'm here, sir." He hurried around to the other side. "You gave us quite a scare, Coach."

The beginnings of a smile flitted across his lips. "K-keep you on toes..."

She threw Tanner a relieved look. "It's good to know you haven't lost your sense of humor, Dad."

"Bakeree..."

"Everything at Madeline's is under control." She smiled through her tears. "Tanner has taken good care of me while you kept Dr. Singh busy."

"My boyzzz..."

She propped her hand on her hip. "Dad, you are not to give football another thought until you're better."

His breathing became slightly more rapid. "Game..."

She pursed her lips. "The game can be rescheduled. Your health is more important than any football game."

"Can't schedule. No forfeit..." Becoming agitated, her father tugged at her hand. "Boys lose chance..."

She looked at Tanner. "Nothing is more important than his health. Certainly not a silly football game."

Her father pulled away. "No."

"Dad!"

"Coach isn't wrong, Maddie." Tanner rubbed the back of his neck. "The game probably couldn't be rescheduled. Truelove would have to forfeit. That would end their chances to make the playoffs."

"You're absolutely no help at all." Glowering at him, she threw out her hands. "The game is the day after tomorrow. The doctor isn't letting you out of the hospital. I don't see that the team has much choice other than to forfeit."

Her father turned to Tanner. "You coach..." Coach's grip was surprisingly strong. "For me... Please."

Tanner shot Maddie a panicked look. "I—I can't. I'm not a coach. I'm not you."

"Be you." Coach shook his head as if to clear his vision. "Principal Moore fix."

Maddie's lips tightened. "Dad, you need to remain calm."

The coach's gaze beseeched him. "Boys deserve chance like you."

Easing free of Coach's grip, Tanner scrubbed his hand over his face.

Maddie's lips quivered. "Tanner? Could you stand in for Dad on Friday? Please?"

He could have refused one of them. But he didn't stand a chance against the both of them. Especially when she looked at him like that. Like he was her only hope.

"I'll stand in for one game, Coach. But the school will need to find a long-term replacement."

Her father's eyes drifted shut. "Th-thank..."

The nurse entered the room. "I think it's time we let your father rest now."

Maddie planted a quick kiss on her dad's forehead. Coach didn't stir.

The nurse herded them toward the elevator. "He'll be more alert the next time you see him."

Gobsmacked by the turn of events, Tanner jabbed the elevator button. What had just happened?

"Thank you for putting Dad's mind at ease." Maddie slipped her arm through the crook of his elbow. "This won't be as bad as you're thinking."

He slumped. "No, it'll be worse."

The elevator dinged. The doors slid open, and they stepped inside. He pressed the button to return to the waiting room floor.

"You and Dad and the team went over the plays yesterday."

As the elevator descended, he kept his gaze glued to the numbers counting down the floors.

She caught his hand. "You won't regret this, Tanner."

He already regretted this. For a multitude of reasons. Including whatever had almost happened between them before Dr. Singh returned.

She hugged his arm. "I'll be with you every step of the way. We'll get through the game together, I promise."

His heart hammered. This was not a good idea.

When the doors opened, they were met by the receptionist.

"Thank goodness I found you." Mrs. Puryear wrung her hands. "There's a group of large teenage boys who insist on speaking with their coach. I put them in the waiting room." She bit her lip. "Should I call security?"

"I don't think that will be necessary." Maddie smiled at him. "Do you, Coach Price?"

He scowled, which seemed to heighten the petite pastry chef's amusement.

Maddie patted the older woman's arm. "I think we can take it from here, Mrs. Puryear."

What had he done? No way was this going to end well. For anyone.

But summoning his courage, he stepped inside the waiting room to greet his new team.

Chapter Four

The group of brawny young men surrounded Maddie. Their faces reflected concern for her dad.

"What's happened to Coach?"

"How's Coach Lovett?"

"Is he going to be okay?"

"Guys!" Randall, the team captain, held up his hand. "Give Miss Maddie a chance to tell us."

The team quieted, and she relayed the pertinent details of her father's heart attack, the surgery and his projected recovery process.

"I'm afraid that means his coaching season is over."

Several of the boys blinked rapidly. A few players swallowed hard. Others hung their heads.

"I—I hate to hear that, Miss Maddie," Hurley stammered. "But I sure am glad Coach is going to be okay."

Offensive lineman Hurley, a.k.a. Hurley Burley, was the biggest player on the squad. A real sweetheart, he was also GeorgeAnne Allen's grandson.

"Just because Dad's season has ended doesn't mean yours has to, though." Maddie exchanged a glance with Tanner. "Coach has asked Mr. Price to step in for him at Friday's game."

All eyes focused on him.

Tanner folded his arms across his chest. "Subject to Principal Moore's approval, of course."

DaShonte, the running back, cocked his head. "Principal Moore hates trash-talking Marshall same as us. She won't want to forfeit to them."

Tanner surveyed the group. "Marshall is a tough team, and it's not ideal that practice had to be canceled today. You'll have to work even harder tomorrow."

Randall jutted his jaw. "We're not afraid of hard work, sir."

"If Principal Moore signs off, I expect to see everyone on the field at 2:45 p.m. sharp tomorrow."

"We'll be there."

"Absolutely."

Javier, possibly the fastest wide receiver in the district, said, "I guess Thursday's team-building night is a no go?"

"I think something can be arranged." Maddie sent Tanner a swift glance. "Stay tuned for further details."

Javier put his hand, palm-side down, into the middle of the huddle. "For Coach."

Randall laid his hand on top of Javier's. "For Coach."

One by one, the other guys followed suit. Tanner put his hand on top of theirs last. "For Coach."

"One, two, three," Hurley grunted. The guys knew the drill.

"Let's go," they chorused and lifted their hands into the air.

"Please let Coach know we're thinking of him," DaShonte said.

"And praying for his recovery," Hurley added.

Their concern for her dad, not only for the game, meant a lot to her.

She'd always felt protective of her dad's teams. "Be safe traveling over the mountain in the dark to Truelove."

DaShonte rolled his eyes. "We're seniors." He elbowed Kyle, the kicker, in the ribs. "It's not like we're letting the freshmen drive."

A freshman, Kyle, a.k.a. Snap, grinned. But that was exactly what they were—teenage boys. Big men on campus, senior or freshmen, not a one of them was older than seventeen.

"Right." She whipped out her phone. "I want the names of the drivers, and I'll expect texts from each of you assuring me you've arrived home safely."

"You heard the lady." Tanner gave the players a look. "Names."

Moaning over the injustice, they nonetheless swallowed their pride and complied.

They left, and she placed a call to Principal Moore. She explained her father's wishes, then handed the phone to Tanner.

Fifteen minutes later, he clicked off and returned the cell to her.

"Everything okay?"

"Ms. Moore's on board." He rubbed his jaw. "But there's paperwork I'll need to complete."

She patted his arm. "There's always paperwork."

"I'm meeting her at school tomorrow morning."

Maddie checked for texts and then stashed her phone in her purse.

He leaned against the couch cushion. "Too early yet for the guys to have made it to Truelove?"

She nodded. "They're a great group of boys."

He smiled. "They do your father and Truelove proud."

"Just as you did."

He shrugged. "Once upon a time. Maybe."

"They'll do you proud, too. For the record, you're still making Dad proud. Whatever Friday's outcome."

He snorted. "I'll have you know, Maddie Lovett, when Truelove comes to play, we play to win."

"Tanner Price, the ultimate competitor." She nudged him. "You sound like Dad."

"Which may be the nicest thing anyone has ever said about me."

They smiled at each other.

"You've got a big day tomorrow, Tanner. Maybe the kids aren't the only ones who need some rest."

"I checked with Miss GeorgeAnne. She and Mom are eating dinner together."

Tanner ended up staying with her for the final CICU visit of the evening.

Her dad's eyes were clearer, though still weak. "Is everything sorted for Friday?"

Maddie cut a look at Tanner. "I'll let you field that question."

Tanner went over his conversation with Principal Moore.

While her dad gave him a few pointers on dealing with Marshall, she got an update from the nurse. A few minutes later, she slipped back into the room. No surprise—they were still talking football.

Her father's color was better, but seeing the strong, good man she'd loved and respected her entire life laid low was hard. Tears filled her eyes.

"None of that," her dad growled. He never could stand to see her cry. "When the going gets tough—"

"I know, I know." She dashed the tears from her eyes. "The tough get going."

Her father was every football cliché rolled into one, and then some.

"Considering your before-dawn bakery call..." Her dad squeezed her hand. "Go home."

She planted her hands on her hips. "There's no way I'm leaving you alone in the hospital overnight. The bakery—"

"You won't be allowed to see me overnight anyway." His gaze darted to Tanner. "Would you see that Maddie gets home, son?"

"I'd be happy to drive her home, sir."

She was reluctant, but eventually her father persuaded her to leave. She fell asleep before Tanner could pull out of the hospital parking lot. She awoke as he steered into her driveway.

He let the engine idle. "Welcome back to the land of the living."

Slightly disoriented, she sat up. "Sorry I bailed on you. I hope I wasn't snoring."

"No snores." He chuckled. "Just gentle, very ladylike breathing."

She brushed her hair out of her eyes. "Not exactly a fun ride over the mountain for you."

"I wasn't bored." His eyes flicked to the windshield. "You don't have to entertain me."

"Thank you for bringing me home." She released the seat belt. "I'll be fine now."

He set his jaw. "I won't be, though, until I see you're safe inside the house."

She perched on the edge of the seat. "That's sweet of you, Tanner."

He made a face. "Football players aren't sweet, Mads."

Every time he called her by the endearing little nickname, a thrill went through her. She'd forgotten he used to call her that. There was much that was endearing about Tanner Price.

"Roger that." She gave him a mock salute. "You're not sweet. Just football-tough." Opening the door, she stepped out of the vehicle. "Go to bed and get some sleep."

"As soon as you go inside and lock the door behind you, I will." His brow creased. "Or maybe

I should check everything is okay." He shifted into Park.

"Totally unnecessary. This is Truelove." She shut the door. "Heading inside now. Bye."

On the porch, she let herself into the darkened house.

Flicking on the foyer light switch, she poked her head out the door to wave goodbye to him. But he made no effort to pull away.

Her phone dinged with an incoming text. Not leaving till you check the house.

She texted him back. You don't need to wait—

Her cell dinged. I can sit here all night, Madeline. Check the house.

Tanner Price was as stubborn as her father, but she did a quick sweep of the house, turning on lights as she went.

Five minutes later, she returned to the porch. Coast is clear. Thanks for everything.

Lock the door, Mads.

Chivalry was alive and well in Tanner Price. But stepping inside, she closed the door and secured the bolt.

Twitching aside the curtain in the living room, she gave him a thumbs-up.

Good night, Maddie.

Good night, Tanner.

Maddie kept watch until the red taillights of his vehicle were swallowed by the night.

Smiling, she collapsed into a nearby chair. Such a gentleman. He'd made a horrible day bearable.

He could deny it till the cows came home. But Tanner Price *was* sweet. Very sweet indeed.

She had one more item to take care of before going to bed. The Thursday night pregame dinner must be salvaged for the team.

Kara answered on the first ring. "Is everything okay with Coach? Are you all right? Are you still at the hospital?"

"Whoa." Maddie laughed. "Dad's resting well in CICU. I'm fine, and I'm at home now."

"Shouldn't you be resting, too?"

Maddie glanced at the clock. "Despite a day that felt like it went on forever, somehow it's not even my usual bedtime yet."

"So what's up?"

"I wanted to see if I could place a last-minute catering order for Thursday night."

"With everything that's happened today, are you sure hosting the team at your house is the best idea, Maddie?"

Taken aback, she stared at the cell in her hand for a second. "I just want to make the team-building night as normal as possible for the guys." And Tanner, too.

"What about if we moved the pregame dinner to the Jar?"

Her heart caught in her throat. "Oh, Kara. That would be wonderful, but it would mean so much work for you. I wouldn't want to impose."

"You're not imposing. I offered. Mama G will be thrilled to lend a hand. She lives for this kind of thing."

Maddie could hear the smile in her voice. As a child, Kara had been orphaned and left to fend for herself on the street, and single mom Glorieta Ferguson, the undisputed queen of a renowned North Carolina barbecue chain, adopted her.

"I'll ask Dad MacKenzie if the ROMEOs might also consider helping out."

The ROMEOs—Retired Older Men Eating Out—were a beloved Truelove institution.

Maddie pursed her lips. "If the ROMEOs are on board, the Double Name Club will probably expect to be included, too."

"Good point. I'll reach out to GeorgeAnne."

Maddie blew out a breath. "I can't tell you how much I appreciate this, Kara. You are the dearest friend anyone could ever have."

Kara promised to be in touch with further details so Maddie could alert the team to the change in location.

Lying in bed, staring at the ceiling, Maddie found herself unable to fall asleep. The events of the tumultuous day played on a loop through her brain. Along with thoughts of her father's star ex-quarterback.

Her fifteen-year-old self would have been completely delirious at having spent most of the day in Tanner's company.

Maddie's grown-up self told her to get a grip. And manage any ridiculous expectations.

She'd always been way more into him than he was into her. He didn't see her as anything but Coach's little daughter. Today had been about him being nice. After Friday's game, she would most likely never see him again.

Finally, emotionally and physically exhausted, she drifted to sleep.

When she dragged herself out of her warm bed the next morning, 5:00 a.m. felt earlier than it usually did. Aghast at her image in the bathroom mirror, she remembered to apply a touch of mascara and a dab of lip gloss.

Just in case Tanner made a pastry run.

Her hair was its usual disaster zone. Pulling the tangle of curls away from her face, she secured it into a messy bun.

Jumping into the vintage light blue VW Beetle she'd inherited from her mom, she headed to the bakery. Having left the place a total mess yesterday, she was pleasantly surprised to find the bakery spotless and ready for baking operations to commence.

Thank you, Kara.

As it turned out, Tanner was not her first customer. Thanks to the Truelove grapevine, though, everyone in town stopped by for a pastry and to express heartfelt wishes for her father's speedy recovery.

It was one of the things she loved most about her hometown—how people supported one another. Of course, the downside was everyone also knew everyone else's business.

As the early-morning rush calmed down by midmorning, Tanner didn't make an appearance. He'd had an appointment with the principal. She tried not to worry that something might be wrong.

When she called the hospital for an update on her dad, the RN on duty informed her he was due to be transferred out of CICU to a regular room soon.

She'd no sooner gotten off the phone than the bell over the door jangled. Her heart leaped. Tanner?

Hurrying to the front of the store, she discovered Kara on the other side of the bakery case.

Reining in her disappointment, she waved her cell in the air. "Dad's getting sprung from CICU."

"That's terrific news." The elegant blond chef threw her a smile. "And how are you?"

To her horror, Maddie burst into tears.

Kara came around the counter and opened her arms. "Oh, honey."

After sobbing briefly on her shoulder, Maddie pulled herself together. "I'm sorry for being so unprofessional."

Kara kept an arm around her. "I'm impressed you opened for business at all. If Mama G was in the hospital, I'd be a basket case."

She tugged Kara toward a table. "Shouldn't you be sitting down?"

"Don't you start, too." But she allowed Maddie to guide her into a chair. "I'm pregnant, not an invalid."

"You and everyone else." Maddie waggled her eyebrows. "So many baby showers coming up... I'll be making petit fours in my sleep."

"Baby showers are good for business." Kara laid a hand on her softly rounded belly. "It must be something in the water."

It was true. Kara's baby shower was next month. The police chief's wife and Shayla Morgan, the wife of a local Christmas tree farmer, were also expecting.

Maddie cocked her head. "Can I get you a coffee or tea?"

"I'm decaf for the duration." Kara loved fancy coffees. "But surprise me with something wonderful."

When she'd remodeled the Mason Jar, Kara was the first to bring lattes, cappuccinos and espresso to Truelove. She'd suggested it might be a smart business move for Maddie to add a similar machine to the bakery. As usual, Kara's business instincts were on the money.

Madeline's professional barista-style machine, complete with a froth steamer wand, was a work of stainless steel art. Along with the cinnamon rolls, a coffee from Madeline's had become the guilty pleasure her customers hadn't known they wanted but now had to have on a daily basis.

Maddie edged around the display case. "Hot apple cider tea work for you?"

"Yum." Kara threw her a smile. "In honor of the season, how about an apple scone, too?"

Known for its apple orchards, Truelove's apple festival was in a few weeks.

Maddie filled a small teapot with hot water and added a loose tea blend of aromatic apples and cinnamon. "Apples remind me of yet another baby shower on my baking calendar—Callie McAbee's." Her family owned Apple Valley Orchard.

Kara rubbed the small of her back. "I hear one of Coach's former players is going to sub for him at Friday's game."

Maddie plated a tray with the steaming teapot, cup, saucer and the flaky apple scone. "That's right."

"Anyone I know?"

Balancing the tray, she set it on the table. "I don't think so." She slipped into a chair across from her business partner.

Kara's eyes widened. "Is that a maple glaze on the scone?"

Maddie grinned at her murmurs of delight. "Tanner Price hasn't lived in Truelove for nine years."

While she brought Kara up to date on her father's recovery, her friend inhaled the scone.

Maddie arched her eyebrow. "I take it you liked the scone?"

"Hey, I'm eating for two." Smiling, the mother-to-be poured herself a cup of tea. "Tell me why your voice changes when you say his name."

Maddie folded her arms across her apron. "My voice does not change when I say Tanner's name."

"You did it again," Kara teased. "So you like this Tanner?"

She sniffed. "Everyone likes Tanner."

Kara batted her eyelashes. "But you *like* him."

"I do not."

Kara smirked. "I get the sense there's more to your relationship than you're letting on." She leaned forward. "Spill it, girl."

Maddie lifted her chin. "There's nothing to tell."

"Nope. Not buying it."

"I had a crush on him in high school, but it was totally unreciprocated on his part."

"But now that he's back…"

Maddie shook her head. "Only temporarily. After Friday's game, he's leaving again." She flipped a curl over her shoulder to illustrate how little she cared. "I have far too much to do to pursue a relationship, anyway."

"That's actually the reason I stopped by." Kara straightened. "What about hiring a part-time employee for Madeline's?"

Maddie's heart sank. "You don't think I'm doing a good job?"

"You're doing a fabulous job. The business is thriving." Kara reached across the table and found Maddie's hand. "But you're already stretched so thin. With your dad ill, it might be something to consider. You could concentrate on what you love the most—baking. And someone else could run the front of the store, leaving you free to help him."

Maddie grimaced. "Who would want to work the hours I do?"

"I would."

She blinked at her friend. "But...you've already got plenty on your plate."

"I've worked myself out of a job at the Jar. These days there's not much for me to do other than consult with Leo about the week's menu."

Kara had mentored her former short-order cook into becoming a culinary chef in his own right.

"My manager, Trudy, has everything under control." Kara gestured. "I need a new challenge."

The bakery wasn't Kara's only business partnership. She also catered events at Birchfield, a 1920s ex–timber baron's country-house venue she co-owned with Kelsey McKendry.

"What about Maddox, Kara?"

After marrying Truelove's fire chief, Kara'd also become a mother to his young son.

Kara smiled. "According to Maddox, second graders don't need their mommies as much. After I drop him off at school, I could work the front for you and then close at three before I head to car pool again."

Maddie shook her head. "I can't see Will thinking much of this plan."

"As long as I bring home pastries, I don't think

he'll mind." She pursed her lips. "Having good work to do would make the time pass faster until my due date."

Maddie threw a pointed look at Kara's belly. "Then what will happen to Madeline's?"

"I think I have a long-term solution. Chloe's parents have decided to permanently return to Truelove to be closer to their family. Her mother, Ann Randolph, is looking for a part-time job. We could rotate days. She'd be perfect for Madeline's."

"You know this, how?"

Kara fiddled with the zipper on her jacket. "Ann told her best friend, Myra Penry, who told her Aunt IdaLee—"

Maddie groaned. "The Double Name Club is involved in this?"

"It's not what you think."

Maddie crossed her arms. "I think every time the matchmakers get involved, mayhem erupts."

"I said the Double Name Club, not the Truelove Matchmakers." Kara cut her eyes at Maddie. "Interesting how you went there, though." She eyed Maddie over the rim of her cup. "That have anything to do with Tanner Price?"

At the sound of the bell, Maddie whirled around. When Tanner walked into the bakery, her heart did a strange uptick.

His gaze darted between her and Kara. "Uh, hey, Maddie."

She fought a valiant fight to regulate her heartbeat. "Hey, Tanner."

Kara choked off a laugh.

Her cheeks went crimson. *Oh, wow.* She *did* say his name different.

Tanner took a step back. "Did I come at a bad time, Mads?"

Eyebrow arching at "Mads," Kara threw Maddie a slightly wicked smile. "Absolutely not. It's Tanner, right?"

"Kara..." Maddie warned.

Ignoring her, Kara sent him a winsome smile. "I can't tell you how pleased I am to finally meet you. I've heard so much about you from Maddie."

"Kara..." she whispered.

For someone so great with child, Kara managed to get up from the chair fairly rapidly.

She approached Tanner, hand outstretched. "I want to thank you for stepping in for Coach."

"Sure." His gaze pinged between the women. "And you are?"

"Just think of me as Maddie's surrogate big sis and business partner."

Maddie glared. "My not-so-silent business partner."

"She told me how much your support has meant to her."

Eyes welling, Kara fanned her face. "She's so dear to me."

He frowned. "Is everything okay, ma'am?"

She fluttered her hand. "I blame pregnancy hormones. I cry over the silliest things."

Reddening, his gaze flicked to Maddie. "Ummm..."

Kara pushed a startled Tanner into her vacated seat. "Would you like a maple scone?"

"I stopped by to get an update on Coach." He sniffed the air appreciatively. "But I wouldn't say no to a scone."

"As Madeline's new part-time employee..." Kara shoved Maddie into the other chair. "I'll get that for you and leave you kids to chat." She beat a hasty retreat behind the display case.

He leaned forward. "Is she always this..."

"Nuts?"

His lips curved. "I was going to say *enthusiastic*."

"Maybe it's a nesting thing?" Maddie rolled her eyes. "She's decided I need looking after while Dad recovers. She's hired herself and Chloe Randolph's mom to be my part-time helpers at the bakery."

"It's about time somebody took care of you." He flushed. "I mean, you've looked after your dad and his teams most of your life." He cleared his throat. "How is Coach?"

She gave him the latest news. "Since Kara has made herself available to close the store, I'll probably head over to the hospital soon and make sure he's settled into his new room. How did things go with the principal?"

"Ms. Moore got the police chief to expedite my background check for tomorrow's game."

Kara bustled over with a scone for Tanner and a mint tea for Maddie. "Our town loves its high school football. Which is probably why Bridger got involved."

Tanner looked at Maddie. "Isn't the police chief Tom Arledge?"

She shook her head. "Chief Arledge retired. His son-in-law, Bridger Hollingsworth, is the new police chief."

Kara nodded. "Tom's a ROMEO now."

Tanner chuckled. "Those old guys still meet at the Mason Jar?"

Kara shook her finger at him. "Don't let them hear you call them 'old.' And yes, they do. My father-in-law, Rick MacKenzie, is also a ROMEO."

"Fire Chief MacKenzie's retired, too?"

Kara's lips twitched. "It's been a minute since you were last in Truelove, hasn't it? My husband, Will, is now the fire chief."

"Fire chief and police chief—keeping it in the family." He laughed. "Only in Truelove."

Maddie sipped her tea. "Without an assistant coach, Dad relies on their support. Every Friday, Rick MacKenzie and Dwight Fleming, another ROMEO, mark the football field for the game."

"The ROMEOs will be there for you, too, Tanner." Kara tapped her chin. "Let me make some calls. I'm sure I can recruit a few volunteers to help you at practice this afternoon."

"I appreciate that." He sat back. "They'd also be a big help to Coach's long-term substitute."

At the pointed reminder, Maddie set the tea mug

on the table with a thud. Kara told him about the change in venue for tonight's dinner.

"That sounds wonderful, Mrs. MacKenzie."

"Handsome and polite." She nudged Maddie. "Please call me Kara, Tanner."

Tightening her grip around the mug, Maddie said nothing.

His eyes cut to her. "Dessert is on me. I'll pick up something at the supermarket."

"Store-bought cookies?" She went rigid. "Absolutely not."

"But with your father in the hospital, you don't—"

"It's a tradition." Maddie ran the ingredients in her supply room through her head. "I have an extra-special treat in mind. I'll drop it off this afternoon at the Mason Jar."

"Oh." He rose. "Then I don't guess I'll—we'll—see you for dinner."

Kara threw her a wide-eyed, innocent look. "I'm sure *everyone* would feel better having you there, Maddie. Isn't that right, Tanner?"

Since when had Kara decided to throw her lot in with the matchmakers?

"It won't be the same without you." Kara gave her an overly bright smile. "Can we count on you at the Jar tonight, Maddie?"

Standing next to the table, Tanner waited for her to answer.

For the love of an eclair... They were ganging up on her.

Bowing to the inevitable, she glowered at her dearest friend and mentor. "I'll be there," she muttered.

He smiled that slow, crooked smile of his. "Great."

Maddie's heart did a treacherous flutter against her rib cage.

Drawn to the window after he exited, she watched him drive away.

Coming alongside her, Kara laughed. "Girl, you've got it bad."

Yes, she did.

And when Tanner left town after the game? Like nine years ago, she'd be in a world of hurt once again.

Chapter Five

Kara followed through on recruiting a few of the ROMEOs. That afternoon, practice went well.

GeorgeAnne's gentleman friend, Walter, a retired judge, and Bill, a retired school administrator, helped Tanner put the team through their paces.

Sticking with Coach's usual schedule, the day before a game was a walk-through practice.

With the guys outfitted in shorts, jerseys and helmets only, Tanner and the ROMEOs rotated between the defensive squad, the offensive line and, finally, the specialty group.

Later, in the locker room, he gazed at the teenage boys. He was slowly getting a handle on their personalities, but he wouldn't be with them long enough to gain a proper understanding of their strengths and weaknesses.

His regret surprised him.

"I assume y'all got the text about Mrs. MacKenzie hosting us at the Mason Jar tonight?"

Randall nodded. "Yes, sir."

The guys had been responsive to every suggestion he made. They were polite, respectful and determined to win. Tomorrow night, the guys would give their all for Coach. Tanner and his teammates would have done the same.

"Coach Lovett will be proud when I tell him about your effort this afternoon." Crossing his arms, he widened his stance. "I'll see you at six thirty at the Jar for team-building night."

"You mean *pasta-building* night." Hurley rubbed his belly. "I can't wait."

Laughing, the guys filed out to shower and change. Tanner thanked Walter and Bill for their assistance. "Any chance you could join me on the sidelines for the game?"

Bill, long-time beau to matchmaker ErmaJean Hicks, slapped him on the back. "You can count on us, Coach Price."

Tanner hurried home to get ready before meeting the team at the diner.

His mother waited for him at the door. "Hi, honey."

The familiar anxiety built in his chest. He peered at her for telltale signs she'd been drinking, but she appeared sober. "Aren't you working the evening shift tonight?"

"I've got a surprise for you."

His gut knotted. With his mom, surprises were usually never a good thing.

But, eyes bright, she drew him into the kitchen. "My turn to cook, and I've made your favorites for dinner."

Over the last few days, he'd made sure she ate

regular, nutritious meals. Although still thin, she was better in every way—physically, emotionally and mentally.

The table was loaded with food. "How did you do this? What about your job?"

She patted his cheek. "I worked split shift at the pharmacy so I could prepare this for you."

His heart sank. She had no idea about the team dinner awaiting him at the Mason Jar.

She pointed out the dishes. "My roast with pepperoncini. Smashed potatoes. Glazed carrots."

He couldn't remember the last time his mother had cooked, much less put together a feast like this.

"Your favorite dessert, too." Her smile was wide. "A peanut butter pie for my peanut butter boy."

She'd called him that when he was little because he wanted peanut butter on everything.

At his lack of enthusiasm, her shoulders slumped. "Unless these aren't your favorites anymore?"

He'd eat two dinners in as many hours before he'd disappoint her. She was trying hard to make things up to him. To be his mom again.

Tanner pulled out a chair. "Can I start with the pie first?"

Her smile lifted her face. "Dinner first, then dessert." Sitting across from him, she placed a generous portion of roast on his plate and generous helpings of the side dishes, too.

His eyelids stung. "This is wonderful."

"You haven't tasted it yet." She made a shooing motion. "Dive in."

"I've started thanking God for the food before I eat." He wasn't sure how she would respond. "Would you pray with me, Mom?"

A hint of confusion gleamed in her eyes. "Whatever you want."

He reached for her hand and bowed his head. "Father God, thank You for this delicious bounty we're about to partake of. Please bless the hands that prepared it. Amen."

Opening his eyes, he found her studying him.

"My dad used to pray for me." She knotted her fingers in her lap. "He was a good man. Like you."

Her parents hadn't approved of Tanner's charming, irresponsible father. When she married him, she'd walked away from her family. They'd been right about his dad.

But her estranged parents had died without Tanner ever meeting them. Only after the divorce had she returned with her young son to Truelove and the house she inherited.

Suddenly, he viewed the home he'd been raised in with fresh eyes. *Thank You, God.* Without this house, he and his mother might have been homeless.

"The food looks great." Gratitude filled his heart. "You look great, Mom."

"I feel great." The candlelight caught glimmers of silver in her blond hair. "I'm better when you're home, Tan-Tan."

Guilt stabbed his chest. Had his absence contributed to her downward spiral? The familiar need to rescue his mom choked his enjoyment of the meal.

"I'm not an alcoholic." She raised her glass to him. "Water, not vodka. I can stop drinking anytime I choose."

"Have you?" Hope welled in his heart. "Stopped drinking for good?"

She set down the glass. "I'm turning over a new leaf. Starting now."

Over the years, she'd made similar promises. He so wanted to believe this time she meant it. That this would be the moment she changed from a self-destructive woman into the loving, kindhearted mother of his childhood.

And because he wanted to believe—that was what faith was all about, wasn't it?—he took her at her word.

Over the next half hour, they talked as they hadn't in years.

He'd feared grief and betrayal had forever erased the lovely, slightly glamorous SandraLynn, who had once been Truelove's sweetheart.

After dinner, he helped her put the kitchen to rights. Blowing him a quick kiss, she left to finish her shift.

He hurried to shower and change clothes. Fifteen minutes later, he drove to the Mason Jar.

Rounding the square, he couldn't help but glance at the darkened interior of Madeline's. His heart swelled at the prospect of seeing the bubbly, energetic pastry chef again.

Like the bakery, the Mason Jar Café typically closed at three o'clock, but tonight it was brimming with life. Streaming into the café, players called out greetings to him.

He nudged Javier with his shoulder. "You clean up pretty good, Diaz."

The wide receiver slicked his shower-damp curly, dark hair off his forehead. "That's what the ladies tell me."

DaShonte snorted. "Dude, the lovely ladies of Truelove High run screaming from your ugly mug straight to me."

A fair amount of good-natured trash-talking and one-upmanship ensued. Chuckling, Tanner allowed them to precede him into the diner. The guys claimed the booths, which overlooked the square.

"Tanner." Retired fire chief Rick MacKenzie threw up his hand. "Welcome." Notepad in hand, he and fellow ROMEOs took beverage orders from the team.

It was Tanner's first time back at the iconic Truelove diner.

"Hey, Coach." Perched on one of the cherry-red swivel stools bolted to the black-and-white-tile floor, Kara sighed. "I've been exiled from the kitchen by my mom."

Supervising the organized chaos, the stout African American woman in a fluttery scarf motioned him toward the lone unoccupied table under the community bulletin board along the far wall. "Take a seat. We're about to start serving."

The table had always been Double Name Club territory. Operation central of the Truelove grapevine.

He folded his arms across his dress shirt. "I can't sit there."

"Of course you can." Diminutive Miss IdaLee, the oldest of the matchmakers, pushed him into one of the chairs. "You are our very welcome guest."

An elderly gentleman, older than IdaLee, shuffled over. "My bride tells me I'm your server tonight."

IdaLee's unusual violet-blue eyes sparkled. "I don't believe you've met my husband, Charles."

She'd taught at least four generations of Truelove children, including Tanner and his mother.

"We were long-lost sweethearts." Charles nodded. "The destination was all the sweeter for the journey it took to find each other again."

IdaLee blushed a becoming shade of pink. "I should help Glorieta."

Tanner rose. "I can help, too."

"Nonsense." IdaLee gave him the teacher look that had quelled many a rambunctious youth. "The Double Name Club has everything under control."

"But—"

Charles clamped a frail hand atop his shoulder. "Resistance is futile, son. I'll get you a sweet tea."

GeorgeAnne and her double-named cohorts bustled through the swinging door from the kitchen to the dining area.

Having the large table to himself, he did a surreptitious scan of the crowd for Maddie.

She'd been headed to the hospital. In the dark, the winding road over the mountains from the county seat was not for the faint of heart. Had something happened with Coach?

Or to her?

His chest tightening, he was about to send her a text when she breezed into the diner laden with a large white bakery box. He did a double take.

She wore a navy-blue print dress, gathered at the waist. Above a pair of tan ankle boots, the hem flirted with her bare calves. Had he ever seen Maddie in a dress before?

Most definitely not, or he would have remembered. His face grew warm. Wouldn't he?

Her hair—that impossibly curly beautiful, dark hair of hers—hung to her shoulders.

She was not the same awkward fifteen-year-old he'd known. He had an uncomfortable sinking suspicion she might not prove as easy to walk away from this time.

Across the café, Maddie's gaze found his. With a slight smile, she broke eye contact and made a point of greeting each of the players scattered throughout the booths.

In her usual forthright manner, GeorgeAnne called the group to order and cued Tanner. Rising, he thanked the Mason Jar and Kara for hosting the team. He also thanked the ROMEOs and the Double Name Club for putting the pregame night together.

The ROMEOs brought out platters piled high with steaming meatballs, spaghetti and stuffed manicotti. Delicious aromas of tomato and garlic filled the diner. His stomach groaned. He steeled himself for discomfort.

GeorgeAnne sat beside him. "SandraLynn told me about her surprise dinner. I didn't have the heart to discourage her. I haven't seen her that happy in a long time."

"Me, either."

"You were a good son to eat with her." She folded her gnarled hands on the tabletop. "I've warned Charles your nerves won't allow you to eat much."

Tanner surveyed the boys, chowing down like they hadn't eaten in weeks. "You're not entirely wrong."

"Once the game kicks off, your instincts will take over. Back in your element, you'll be fine."

He blew out a breath. "I wish I had your confidence."

She patted his arm. "Did you leave any room for dessert?"

"If it's from Madeline's, I'll make room."

His gaze pinged around the room. Somehow he'd lost track of Maddie. Had she left already?

"In case you were wondering, Maddie is in the kitchen, plating cake."

He flushed.

"It's a red velvet cake in honor of the team colors." GeorgeAnne chortled. "I hope cake isn't the only thing you'll make room for in your life."

Tanner scowled. "Don't start, Miss GeorgeAnne... I'm not in the market for anything other than cake."

"Heard that before." The older woman smirked. "I'll look forward to watching you eat crow."

Maddie brought Tanner's cake to him. Mr. Charles could have done the honors, but she hadn't talked to Tanner in at least four hours.

Yes. She was that pathetic. But if there was one thing she felt confident in, it was the ability of her cakes to please.

She'd also made every effort to look her best tonight. She'd put on makeup. And worn her favorite soft boho-style dress.

"You wanted to taste test a special occasion cake." She set the plate in front of him. "Voila!"

Grimacing, he pushed the plate away.

Her breath hitched. "Is something wrong with the cake?"

"Noooo... ." He heaved a sigh. "I just don't think I should eat anything right now."

He appeared green around the gills.

"Are you feeling okay?"

Slipping into the seat next to him, she placed her hand on his forehead. His eyes went wide. A muscle jerked in his cheek.

Maddie immediately dropped her hand. "I'm sorry."

What had she been thinking? Reacting in concern, she *hadn't been* thinking. Her gaze cutting right, then left, she hoped none of the boys—or worse, the matchmakers—had witnessed her gesture.

She reached for the plate. "If you don't want the cake—"

Tanner's hand shot out and took hold of the plate. "I do want the cake."

She didn't let go of the plate and neither did he. "What's wrong, Tanner?"

"My stomach's unsettled. Probably nerves." He winced. "All of a sudden, it's gotten real that I'm coaching a football game tomorrow night. I don't want to let everyone down."

"You won't. I have total faith you'll rise to the occasion." She winked. "'Occasion'? You see what I did there?"

His eyes crinkled. "Like the cake. I got it, Mads."

She flicked a long, curly strand of hair over her shoulder. "Besides, it's not about whether we win or lose but how we—"

"Are you kidding me, Madeline Lovett?" Letting go of the plate, he gaped at her. "Football is all about winning."

"Of course it is, Coach Price." She fluttered her lashes at him. "Silly me."

His mouth curved. "What would your father say to such sacrilege?"

"Dad would probably disown me."

He fingered his jaw. "Since we can't allow that, looks like there's no other choice but to win."

She steepled her hands on the table. "Exactly."

He threw her a sheepish look. "Perhaps you ought to be the one giving the pep talk before the game."

She smirked. "I think you've got it covered."

He took a breath. "I don't know how I would do this without you."

If only he wasn't so determined to leave after the game.

"What's going through that pretty head of yours, Maddie?"

Tanner Price thinks I'm pretty?

"Ummm..." *Words, Maddie. Use your words.* "I should..."

"Can I save my cake for later?" He smiled. "As a reward. After Truelove shows Marshall where football really lives."

"Sure, I'll wrap it up for you."

His blue eyes clouded. "You'll be at the game, won't you?"

She clutched the plate. "Would you like me to be?"

"It would mean a lot, knowing I had someone cheering me on."

She suddenly realized that in all the years he'd played ball at Truelove High, he'd never had anyone attend a game on his behalf.

Her heart turned over at the earnest expression on his face. "Of course I'll be there, Tanner. I wouldn't miss it for the world."

The next evening, she huddled under a heavy

blanket on the high school bleachers with Kara, her family and other die-hard Truelove High football fans.

Right before kickoff, Tanner turned toward the spectators. His brow furrowed, but then his gaze connected with hers, and something in his features eased.

With a small nod, he focused on the field once more. But it was enough. Because he knew she was there for him.

Guiding the team to victory, he proved to be more than a capable substitute coach. Truelove High didn't just win—they thoroughly trounced Marshall.

At the end of the game, the teams shook hands in a gesture of good sportsmanship.

Tanner was surrounded by happy Truelove football supporters who rushed to congratulate him. He caught Maddie's eye.

Burger Barn? he mouthed.

She nodded. Per Truelove tradition, the celebration after a home game was always at the Burger Barn on the highway outside town. She'd catch up with him there.

Leaving him to his legion of fans, she said goodbye to the MacKenzies and headed for her car.

Storing the equipment and shutting down the field would take a while. She had time to run an errand or two before Tanner and the team arrived at the hamburger joint.

Her dad was scheduled to be transported to the

acute-care facility early next week. He'd asked her to pack him a small duffel bag with toiletries.

With the Truelove pharmacy long-since closed for the evening, she'd have to shop at the larger pharmacy in the strip mall on the highway.

At the store, she pulled up the list her dad had texted and scouted the aisles. Shaving lotion—check. Deodorant—check. Eau de toilette spray for men—

Since when did her dad wear anything but Old Spice? And why did he need cologne for the rehab center?

A clerk had to unlock the men's fragrance cabinet. The clerk—a woman she recognized from church—took her time before handing it to Maddie. "Your boyfriend's gonna love this. And you can enjoy how nice he smells, sugar pie."

Heat engulfed her chest. After paying, she headed for the exit at a run. She'd hoped to hit the big-box store across the parking lot for a few baking supplies, but with a swift glance at the time, she abandoned the idea.

At the stoplight, a car resembling SandraLynn Price's white sedan stopped in front of her. When the car turned left, she caught a glimpse of the driver. It was indeed Tanner's mom.

SandraLynn must have just gotten off shift at the pharmacy. Maddie prayed his mother hadn't overheard the clerk's remarks.

For Tanner's sake, she hoped his mother was on her way to celebrate his triumph with the rest of the town. But SandraLynn made a right turn onto a different road.

Driving past, Maddie didn't see where his mother went, but there were only two establishments on that street. An industrial park. And the local liquor store.

Her stomach clenched. Surely not. Yesterday, Tanner had mentioned how his mother was turning her life around.

But unease nagged at Maddie. At the restaurant, the gravel lot was almost full. The fans and players had beaten her there.

Hands stuffed in his pockets, Tanner stood outside the entrance. After spotting her, he came over and opened her car door. "Is everything all right?"

Shaking off her misgivings about his mother, she got out. "Had to pick up some items for Dad."

"Oh." He crimped the bill of his Truelove Bobcat baseball cap. "I wondered if you'd changed your mind about coming." He crossed his arms in that feeling-insecure body language of his.

Reaching for his hands, she forced his arms open. "I told you I'd be here." She smiled at him. "Congratulations. I'm so proud of you, Coach Price."

He gave her a small smile. "The team did Truelove proud."

"You did Truelove proud, too."

His gaze flicked to her Truelove High Bobcat sweatshirt. "Your hands are ice cold. You should've worn a coat and gloves."

Tanner warmed her hands with his. When he

looked at her with something more than fondness in his eyes, her heart took flight.

"Maddie, I—" He swallowed, hard.

Leaning on the tips of her boots, she lifted her face. "Yes?"

His lips parted. Her breath caught.

"Maddie," he rasped. "I need to tell you—"

A horn blared.

She put her hand to her throat. "What did you want to tell me, Tanner?"

He scrubbed his hand over his face. "Now, with the game over, I'll be leaving on the first flight I can book."

Stupid, delusional Maddie. When would she get it through her head that Tanner Price had never and would never be into her?

Don't make a bigger idiot of yourself than you already have.

She took a deep breath. "This is goodbye, then?"

He scuffed the gravel with his work boot. "I guess so."

She tucked an errant strand of hair behind her ear.

For a split second, his eyes flashed. Then he looked away. "Have yourself a wonderful life, Maddie."

Willing herself not to cry, she bit her lip. "I hope your life, Tanner, becomes everything you most long for."

"Maddie."

Dodging his hand, she slipped into her car.

He blinked. "You don't have to go."
Yes, she did.
"Goodbye," she whispered.
She took one last look in the rearview mirror. Staring after her car, he remained where she'd left him.
Her heart aching, she drove away.

Chapter Six

Later, when Tanner left the Burger Barn and went home, he found the house dark. His mother's car was exactly where it had been when he left earlier to go to the game. But some instinct made him put his hand on the engine hood.

It was warm.

After the wrenching goodbye with Maddie, any remaining good feelings from the win over Marshall evaporated.

Where had his mother been while he was at the football game? She'd worked the day shift.

Of course, there was no reason why she shouldn't have gone out. She was a grown woman, not a child who had to account for her whereabouts at all times.

But Friday nights had usually been when her weekend binges began.

His suspicions aroused, he went into the house expecting to find his mother passed out in her recliner. But after flipping on the overhead kitchen light, he found his favorite candy bar and a note on the table.

The Christmas Playbook

Congratulations on your victory, Coach Price!

She'd heard about the win and gone to the grocery store. The relief buckled his knees.

He sank into one of the chairs at the kitchen table. He dropped his head into his hands. He hated doubting her, though in the past such suspicions had been well-founded.

She'd promised him she'd stopped drinking. Instead of expecting her to fail, he needed to see all the ways she was trying to succeed.

His mother needed him to believe in her. He glanced at the chocolate bar. Like she'd always believed in him.

Tanner had intended to save the red velvet cake as a reward for winning the game. But saying goodbye to Maddie had been harder than he'd anticipated. He didn't have the heart to eat her cake.

Going to bed, he immediately fell into a deep slumber. Hours later, he awoke to sunshine streaming into his bedroom.

For a few minutes, he lay there, reliving last night's win. He hadn't felt a part of something like that since he'd stopped playing football. The town's support had been surprising and heartwarming.

He stared at the ceiling. With his mom on the road to recovery and the game against Marshall won, there wasn't much to keep him in Truelove.

Except for Maddie.

Tanner glanced at the clock on the nightstand. *Whoa.* Throwing aside the cover, he rolled out of bed. Had he really slept until noon?

Barefoot, he stumbled into the kitchen to find his mother making pancakes.

Spatula in hand, she turned. "Congratulations on the win. I never doubted the outcome for an instant."

Unlike how he'd doubted her last night. Not his finest moment.

He scraped his hand over his stubble. "Thanks for the chocolate, Mom, but you didn't have to make a special trip to get it."

She flipped a pancake. "It's no trouble to celebrate my son's success." Glancing over her shoulder, she winked. "You up for a breakfast of champions?"

"I could eat."

She hugged him. "Some things never change."

His mom smelled of maple syrup. He hated the instant relief he felt. What had he expected? Cigarettes and booze?

Trust her. Stop being so paranoid. But the ingrained habits of a lifetime were hard to break.

Over pancakes, she asked for details on the game. He gave her a short rundown of the highlights.

She toyed with her napkin. "I suppose with your commitment to Coach at an end, you'll return to your job?"

"I guess so. Since you and Coach don't need me anymore."

Her mouth curved downward. "I'll always need you, son, but you have your own life to live." She reached for his empty plate. "No need to worry about me."

But he did. Another ingrained habit. He couldn't shake the feeling she wasn't as fine as she wanted him to believe.

After getting dressed, he was getting out his laptop to search for flights to the UK when the doorbell chimed.

"Tanner?" his mother called. "You've got a visitor."

He surged to his feet. It was Principal Moore.

"Is everything okay?" His heart seized. "Is it Coach?"

Clutching a briefcase, the tall woman shook her head. "Coach is on the mend, but there's something I'd like to discuss with you."

His mother threw him a quizzical look but excused herself to let them talk in private. They sat down in the living room.

Principal Moore set the briefcase at her feet. "I was impressed with how you led the team to victory last night. So was the school board."

"Thank you." He studied the principal. "It was a great experience, coaching the team this week."

"I've been unable to find a replacement coach for the rest of the season. I'm here to ask if you'd consider staying on for however long the team's season continues."

"They're going to make it to the playoffs, Ms. Moore." Leaning forward, he rested his elbows on his knees. "This team—these guys—have a lot of talent and even more heart. They have the potential to go all the way." He shook his head. "But I have a job waiting for me on the other side of the world."

"I understand." She sighed. "Yet without you, their season is over."

"You truly searched for a replacement?"

"It's the larger school districts that attract the most applicants." She folded her hands in her lap. "I've put out feelers with the education departments at Appalachian State and Western Carolina. But any potential candidates wouldn't be able to start until after their mid-December graduation."

He frowned. "After the championship game."

"Exactly."

With the team's future in jeopardy, how could he not stick around and help the guys position themselves for a chance at the playoffs?

"I want to be upfront with you." She looked him in the eye. "Not only do I need to find a football coach, I also need someone to cover Coach's teaching responsibilities."

He balked. "I'm no teacher."

"I've watched you interact with our student athletes." She opened her hands. "Some things can be taught, but for a teacher, there are many important traits that cannot be taught. You possess those traits in abundance."

He frowned. "I might know a thing or two about football, Ms. Moore, but as for the rest... I'm not qualified."

"The school board is prepared to issue you temporary certification. The social science department is willing to divvy up Coach's Civics classes in exchange for you taking over one of the study periods."

He swiped his hand over his head.

"My first priority is always the welfare and education of the children. I wouldn't make this offer unless I truly believed you were the right man for the job."

"Other than football, high school was a nightmare for me. Have you checked my academic record? I'm the last person you should want teaching kids."

"I'm well aware of your learning disability, Tanner. It's because of what you've overcome, rather than in spite of it, which makes me confident I can trust you with my kids."

Shocked at her assessment of him, he stared. "You're serious about this, aren't you?"

The principal inclined her head. "Will you consider my offer?"

What should I do, God?

The microwave beeped in the kitchen.

Of greater importance to him than the team's playoff goals was his mother's well-being. Would remaining in Truelove improve the chances of her continued sobriety?

Thoughts of Maddie also tugged at his heart. His reluctance to say goodbye to her was new. And disconcerting.

Feeling awash in a sea of uncertainty, the unexpected job offer felt like a reprieve. A sign from God? An answer to prayer.

He extended his hand. "I'm willing to give it a try."

She shook his hand. "I'm so pleased. And don't worry. One of our veteran teachers will mentor you." She reached for the briefcase. "I have Coach's lesson plans, student roster and schedule."

The principal laid the paperwork on the coffee table. He joined her on the sofa. For the next thirty minutes, she brought him up to speed.

Despite feeling overwhelmed, a strange excitement began to build in his chest. He wasn't one to back away from a challenge. If he was, he would have never led his team to a football championship or made a successful career for himself.

He saw Ms. Moore out. A floor in the hallway squeaked.

"You can come out now, Ma," he called. "I guess you heard the news."

His mother edged into the living room. "What about your job?"

"I've got a ton of personal leave. I'll make a call." He lifted his chin. "I think the company will work with me."

"So you're staying?"

"Through Christmas, anyway. If it's okay with you. Don't want to wear out my welcome."

"You'll never wear out your welcome with me, Tan-Tan." She hugged him. "This will be the best Christmas ever."

A sudden vision of Maddie rose in his mind. Of her laughing chocolate-brown eyes. Her cheeks rosy from the cold. And mistletoe.

A feeling of rightness settled over him. His mother was right. This was shaping up to be the best Christmas ever.

Saturday morning, Maddie woke not in the greatest of moods. She prided herself on her ever-optimistic attitude. The whole 'when life gives you lemons, make cupcakes' philosophy.

But with Tanner leaving town, her world—Truelove—seemed far less bright.

Unable to pull herself out of the doldrums, she headed to Madeline's for her usual predawn baking. At seven, Ann Randolph arrived to open the storefront to customers. Then Chloe's mom shooed her out.

It was freeing and yet also unnerving to find herself with time on her hands. Knowing her father would be anxious to hear about the game, she headed to the hospital.

She stopped by the nurses' station to get an update.

"Your father is doing well. A positive mental attitude plays an important role in a patient's recovery." Fiftysomething Nurse Crabtree folded her arms across her spotless lavender scrubs. "He also believes it's his personal duty to boost the spirits of every patient on the floor."

Not a surprise to Maddie. Her father was an encourager.

A harried expression crossed the nurse's face. "Our biggest challenge is to get him to rest instead of traipsing up and down the hall visiting his new friends." The woman's lips pursed. "They need their rest, too."

When she ventured into her father's room, his eyes brightened. "There's my favorite girl."

She gave him a quick peck on the cheek. "How are you, Dad?"

"Never better." He rubbed his hands together. "Can't wait to get sprung from here. You wouldn't believe how bossy everyone is."

"You must be feeling better." She planted her hands on her hips. "From what I've heard, you're giving the staff a hard time and not resting enough."

"I suppose Nurse Crabby told on me. No one likes a tattletale, Maddie."

She wagged her finger at him. "If you want to get released any time soon, you have to follow Crabby's—I mean, the nurse's orders."

He grinned.

She fought the urge to smile. "Behave, Dad."

"I want all the details about the game."

She gave him the play-by-play.

"How did Tanner react during his first coaching gig?"

Tanner's first and last coaching gig. Not something her father needed to know. At least, not right now. Otherwise, he'd spend the coming week agonizing over the next game and derail his recovery.

Maybe if she focused on the game, she could divert her dad from awkward questions.

"Tanner did great." She injected as much cheer as she could muster into her voice. She rattled on about a guard on the opposing offensive line who lost his balance, fell forward, got up, ran around the tackle and returned to his spot. "No penalty flag was called."

Her father's eyes narrowed. "How did Tanner handle it?"

"Exactly how you would've." She smiled. "Throughout the game, he showed respect for the refs. Tried not to tick 'em off, and tried to be as likable as possible."

Her father nodded. "Building trust and credibility with the officials. Sometimes it pays off, sometimes it doesn't. What happened?"

"The ref said 'unathletic does not a foul make.'"

Her dad snorted. "The kid's probably his nephew."

In their rural district, it wasn't out of the realm of possibility. "Tanner politely expressed his disagreement but then walked away. He also didn't allow the players to address the ref directly over any missed calls."

"Good man. And the next time there was an issue?"

She smiled. "The ref went Tanner's way."

"Reasonable and strategic. Playing the long

game." Her father leaned against the pillows. "I hoped he might stop by with you."

Dropping her gaze, she rose off the side of the bed. "He's probably exhausted."

"I can't wait to tell him how proud I am of him."

Her gut pinched. For all she knew, Tanner was in an airplane somewhere over the Atlantic Ocean by now. It was time to make a strategic exit before her father pulled the truth out of her.

She'd never been good at hiding anything from him. "I should let you rest."

His face fell. "So soon?"

"The bakery—"

"Of course. Madeline's must be your priority."

Maddie's conscience twinged. "You'll always be my first priority, Dad."

He pulled her into a hug. "It won't be long before I'm home."

A headache teased at the edges of her skull. She wanted nothing more than for her dad to come home. But even with help at the bakery, how would she cope with the added responsibility of his care?

Lest her face betray her conflicted emotions, she said goodbye. At the end of the stark-white corridor, Principal Moore stepped out of the elevator.

The statuesque woman's eyes widened. "Oh, Maddie, dear. I didn't realize you were visiting your father." Her gaze cut to the elevator door, closing slowly behind her. "Perhaps I should—"

"I was just leaving. Dad will be thrilled at the prospect of more company."

She wasn't sure whether he would be pleased or not. Judy Moore had been at the school about five years, but she'd never heard her father say anything about the principal. Which, for as gregarious a man as her dad, was curious.

"I come bearing gifts." The principal held up a white paper bag with the Madeline's logo on it. "Who can resist your cinnamon rolls?"

To the best of her recollection, Principal Moore had never darkened Madeline's doors, much less bought anything. "You like my cinnamon rolls?"

"I do." Principal Moore flushed. "I—I guess I should've realized when you weren't at the bakery, you would be here. With your father."

She'd never seen the strictly business administrator so flustered. *Interesting...*

"It's okay for me to bring Coach a cinnamon roll, isn't it?" The high school principal clutched the bag. "Or is it against doctor's orders?"

A sudden realization struck Maddie. When had her father's usual morning to-go order morphed from one cinnamon roll to two? Had he been sharing them with his boss?

Maddie tucked a curl behind her ear. "I don't think one cinnamon roll—every once in a long while—" she added in the interests of her father's new dietary plan "—will do much harm."

The fiftysomething woman's face brightened.

"Provided the roll was split in half and shared." She looked at the administrator. "Are you willing to share the roll with my father, Ms. Moore?"

"I am, Miss Lovett." The principal's cheeks went pink. "I'd love for you to call me Judy. Your father and I are colleagues but also..." She moistened her lips. "Friends."

Aha! The eau de toilette spray.

Something sweet pinged in her heart. Her dad had been widowed a long, long time. Someone like Judy Moore in her father's life would have made her mother so happy.

"I don't think we've ever been properly introduced, Judy. Please call me Maddie. Your visit is well-timed." She fluttered her hand toward her father's room. "He's driving the nurses bonkers demanding to go home. And when he does, I will have my hands full taking care of him."

"I doubt you'll lack offers to help you manage. ErmaJean Hicks is already making meal train plans. Aunt IdaLee is organizing a visitor rotation to sit with him while you're away from home each day."

"Really?"

God bless Truelove and the endearingly meddlesome Double Name Club. She'd forgotten Judy was one of IdaLee's nieces. She'd never managed to untangle the retired schoolmarm's extensive family tree.

"I'd also like to be there for you and your father." Judy's mouth wobbled. "If you'll allow me, of course."

Truelove would never let one of their own down.

If he'd stuck around long enough, Tanner would have discovered the same.

Maddie kneaded her forehead. She was tired of thinking about Tanner Price. Tired and too sad.

"Thank you, Judy." She hitched the strap of her purse higher on her shoulder. "I look forward to getting to know you better."

A few minutes later, sitting in her car, she rested her throbbing forehead on the steering wheel. What now? She wasn't used to being at loose ends.

She was thrilled for this new romantic development in her dad's life, but it only underscored the lack of it in her own.

What was she waiting for? Should she create a profile on one of those dating apps? Many of her culinary school friends had gone that route. The results had been mixed.

But a future with anyone who didn't live near Truelove was a deal-breaker. Even without Madeline's, she could never contemplate leaving her hometown for good.

Just then, her stomach rumbled with hunger. An early-morning latte and a croissant didn't count as sustenance. Passing the Burger Barn, though, she gave the scene of last night's Tanner debacle a wide berth.

Crossing the bridge onto Main Street, she drove past the Mason Jar. She couldn't risk well-meaning Truelove fans wanting to analyze last night's game—and heaping praise on the substitute coach.

Better to just go home. And eat whatever she could find in the fridge. Alone.

Veering into her driveway, she ground to an immediate halt beside the pickup truck parked next to her house.

Leaning against the vehicle was Tanner.

A ridiculous hope surged in her chest. A hope she did her best to beat into submission. He'd made a point of saying goodbye last night.

Yet she couldn't stop her heart from turning over at the sight of him. Why was he here? What could he possibly want?

Steeling herself against further hurt, she took her time getting out of the car.

Hands stuffed in his pockets, Tanner offered her a tentative smile. "Surprised to see me?"

Baffled, was more like it.

"After Principal Moore left my house, I couldn't wait to tell you."

Judy had been to Tanner's house this morning *and* the bakery? Dad's boss—and love interest—had had quite the morning.

He cocked his head. "I've been waiting for you to come home for hours."

Yeah, well, join the club, buster. She'd been waiting years for Tanner to come home.

Sucking in a breath, she folded her arms over her cardigan. Was that true? She'd first used culinary school and then getting Madeline's established as her excuse for her lack of a social life.

But like Saturday-morning quarterbacking, hindsight was always twenty-twenty.

How stupid was she? Waiting around for years only for him to waltz into town and waltz right back out a week later. Moisture pricked the back of her eyelids.

She mustn't cry in front of him. She'd practically thrown herself at him last night and been thoroughly rejected for her efforts.

Maybe he'd leave quickly—he was good at leaving. Then she'd have the rest of the weekend to cry over him at her leisure.

Swiveling, she gripped her key fob to lock the car. No one locked their vehicles in Truelove. Not that he was sticking around long enough to know that.

"Maddie?"

Buying a few seconds to compose herself, she jabbed the button on the fob. The car locks clicked. "Is there something you needed?" She concentrated on tucking the fob into her purse.

"I *need*..." Exasperation laced his voice. "I'd *like* for you to turn around so I can tell you my news."

She stiffened. News? What news?

"You were the first person I wanted to tell." There was a beat of silence. "Are you not happy to see me again, Mads?" A hint of hurt threaded his voice.

It wasn't in her nature to be mean. Some friend she was—thinking only of herself.

She faced him. "I'm very glad to see you, Tanner.

And very surprised." She was pleased at how normal a tone she managed. "What's the big news?"

"Principal Moore—"

"Why was Judy at your house?"

His eyes narrowed. "Since when are you and Ms. Moore on a first-name basis?"

"Since about an hour ago, when I found out she and Dad are dating."

"Coach and Principal Moore?" he sputtered.

"I know, right?" She flicked a curl over her shoulder. "What did Judy want to see you about?"

"No one else has stepped forward to fill the coaching vacancy."

"I'm sorry to hear that."

Disappointing for the fans, crushing for the guys. But in light of the day's other surprises—like Dad's new girlfriend and Tanner standing in her yard—not that big of a bombshell for her.

"Ms. Moore asked me to coach the guys to the championship." He cut his eyes at her. "I agreed."

She blinked. "Wait, so you're staying?"

"Through the playoffs in December."

Sheer, unadulterated joy rose inside her. Out of a sense of self-preservation, though, she reined in her happiness with a stern dose of reality. He'd only be here through Christmas.

"She also asked me to take over his class schedule. That's the part that scares me the most."

"Civics and Phys Ed."

"Phys Ed and a study hall period I'm responsible

for in exchange for one of the history teachers taking on the Civics classes."

She smiled. "Nothing to worry about. You're great with kids."

"You think so?"

"I think you'd figure out a way to succeed no matter what the challenge."

"Not true." A slow smile curved his lips. "What if, for instance, somebody wanted me to bake a cake?"

She tilted her head. "I think someone like me could help you."

"Or what if the hospital called and asked me to pinch-hit for a neurosurgeon?" His eyebrows rose. "Still think I would succeed?"

She stuck her tongue in her cheek. "Since study hall, football and P.E. aren't brain surgery, I believe you'll be fine."

He grinned. "I can always count on you to talk me off the ledge."

Apparently, she was his go-to, best buddy, favorite gal pal. *Yay, her.*

Some people had comfort animals. If there was such a thing as a comfort baker, she reckoned she'd be his.

Maddie sighed.

"Seriously, though, Mads, I'd like to spend more time with you, but I want to be clear. Anything other than friendship wouldn't be a good idea for either of us." He hunched his shoulders. "That is, if you want to spend time with me."

Behind the tough facade, vulnerability shone from his eyes.

She could no more resist him now than she'd been able to resist the seventeen-year-old Tanner.

He was friend-zoning her. Moving forward, there'd be rules. Got it. She could work with rules.

"I'd like to spend time with you, too, Tanner."

He released a slow breath. "Great."

Spending more time with him wasn't a smart idea. But whatever the sell-by date, she wouldn't—couldn't—pass up the opportunity. Not for all the patisseries in Paris.

Chapter Seven

Standing outside her house, as soon as Tanner realized she hadn't had lunch, he insisted Maddie eat something.

"There's not much in the house." She shrugged. "I meant to go to the grocery store, but between juggling work at Madeline's and getting Dad settled..."

"Isn't there an all-day place on the highway? We could make a grocery run, too."

"We?"

He arched his brow. "Surely you know me well enough to realize I can always eat, Mads?"

She laughed.

He sobered. "One more perk of staying in Truelove is I can be there for you the way you and Coach were always there for me."

"You don't owe us, Tanner."

"Friendship is a two-way street, Maddie. Let me be your friend. Please."

She looked at him a long moment. The girl who wore her heart on her sleeve went uncharacteristically quiet. What was going on behind those big brown eyes of hers?

He felt shut out. And he didn't like it. Not one little bit. Not when it came to her.

Yet, no way could they ever work as a couple, and the last thing he wanted was to lead her on. He hadn't been sure how she would respond to the olive branch of friendship only.

The wind blew a curl across her cheek. His pulse jackhammered.

Brushing it off her face, she lifted her chin. "We can look over Dad's lesson plans while we're at dinner."

Some of the tension he'd been holding on to since last night eased. He smiled. "And I want details about this new development with Coach and Ms. Moore."

The restaurant chain was one of those all-you-can-eat buffet places. No sooner were they seated than Maddie groaned.

"What?"

"Don't look now, but we're not the only ones here for the early bird special."

He started to turn around, but she grabbed his hand. "I told you not to look," she hissed.

"Surest way to get someone to look is to tell them not to. What am I *not* supposed to be looking at?"

Ducking her head, she inched a peek over the top of the booth. "Maybe if we lay low, she won't see us." Maddie darted a glance at him. "If you scrunch those broad shoulders of yours down a tad?"

He stared at her as if she'd lost her mind.

"Oh no. Too late." Her eyes went deer-in-the-headlights. "We've been spotted. She's coming this way."

"Who are you look—" He angled. "Oh, hey, Miss GeorgeAnne. Mr. Walter."

GeorgeAnne tapped her chin with her bony finger, "Fancy finding you two here."

"I'm thrilled you're staying on board the Bobcat Express." Walter thumped him across the back. "You can count on Bill and me to go with you all the way to the championship."

He glanced between the older couple. "You know about that already?"

"Was there ever a doubt?" Maddie muttered. "The Truelove grapevine is real."

GeorgeAnne pursed her lips. "I'm also delighted to learn one of our other projects is finally official."

Maddie gaped at her. "Am I the last to know about my father and Judy Moore?"

GeorgeAnne pushed her cat's-eye glasses higher on the bridge of her nose. "I don't think the infants in Truelove are yet aware."

Tanner laughed. Maddie glared at him.

"Come on, Georgie." Walter tugged at the matchmaker. "Let's leave these two to their meal."

After dinner, Tanner went over a few questions about Coach's school routine with Maddie.

"I meant what I said about getting plugged into the community. Especially a faith community." He bit his lip. "Would you mind if I joined you at church tomorrow?"

For the first time since their talk earlier, her smile felt warm. "Your mom, too?"

"I don't think she'll come, but I'll ask."

Insisting on going Dutch, she handed her credit card to the cashier to split the cost. "Friends pay for their own meals."

Short of risking a scene, there wasn't much he could say. But something about it didn't set right with him.

After a grocery run, he offered to help her unpack the groceries at her house.

"Thanks, but I'm going to make it an early evening." She ushered him to the porch. "Good night, Tanner."

He supposed boundaries went both ways. "Night, Maddie."

Tanner went home to a dark, shuttered house again. This time, his mother's car wasn't in the driveway. He consulted her work calendar, pinned to the inside of the pantry door.

Closing the store tonight, she wouldn't be home for hours. Usually preferring his own company to anyone else's—except Maddie's, maybe?—he pulled out the piece of red velvet cake from the fridge.

Alone in the kitchen, he ate the cake slice. But somehow it didn't taste as fabulous as he'd imagined.

After a restless night, he was pouring himself a cup of coffee when his mom staggered into the kitchen. Was something off with her, or was he being paranoid?

She gathered her bathrobe around her. "Up and at 'em kind of early for a Sunday morning, aren't you?"

He frowned. "Are you feeling okay?"

She waved her hand. "Long shift." Brushing her hair off her forehead, she peered at him. "Why are you so dressed up this morning?"

"I met Pastor Bryant at the hospital this week, and I decided to visit his church this morning." He thrust the coffee mug toward her.

Taking a sip, she closed her eyes. "You're a lifesaver."

"I'd love for you to come with me, Mom."

Her eyes flew open. "To church?" She shook her head. "I don't think so. No one would welcome seeing me."

"GeorgeAnne would. So would Maddie."

"That's why you're really headed to church." She sent him a wry glance. "Although, as reasons go, that's as good a one as any."

He flushed. "I'm not going to church because of Maddie, Mom." He tried to explain what his newfound faith meant to him.

She sniffed. "Since I haven't lived a perfect life, thanks but no thanks. I can do without being preached at."

"Nobody's going to preach at you." This was not going as he'd hoped. "Nobody has lived a perfect life, except for one person. He's the reason why I go."

"I can pray just fine on my shift or in my car or at this table drinking—"

"Coffee?"

He shouldn't have said that.

Spots of temper peppered her pale cheeks. "Despite your sudden moral amnesia, I remember several less-than-stellar incidents of yours involving cheerleaders." Clutching the mug, she stumbled away from him and slammed her bedroom door.

He flinched.

She wasn't wrong about the mistakes he'd made in the past. He'd been a cocky, immature kid catapulted into local fame because of his ability to throw a football. There'd been no one, least of all her, to show him a better way. Although, that was no excuse.

Last year, after putting his trust in God, he'd grieved and sought forgiveness for his wrong choices.

But family had a front-row seat to mistakes. And they never let a person forget it.

He'd let his frustration with his mother boil over. Perhaps he shouldn't go to church today. He was no more worthy than his mother to show his face there.

Yet what had dodging the truth ever done for him? How foolish would he be to refuse to go to the one place that could offer him what he needed the most?

"I'm sorry, God," he whispered.

He'd pushed his mother too hard. If he wanted her to believe he was a changed man, he'd need to be more patient.

It wasn't far to Maddie's church. Nestled in a glade on the edge of town, the white steeple brushed a picture-perfect Blue Ridge sky. A tiny footbridge, spanning the small creek, separated the gravel parking lot from the two-hundred-year-old country church.

Above the soft murmur of human voices were sweet sounds of birdsong, the rustle of leaves in an autumn breeze and the burbling melody of rushing water over moss-covered stones.

Knots of people gathered in front of the sanctuary. He faltered and would have turned back, but Chloe and Noah joined him. They walked with him to where Maddie waited for him at the base of the church steps.

She smiled. "Hi, Tanner."

His heart skipped a beat. Everything wrong with his day suddenly went right. *Oh, Maddie, what are you doing to me?*

Through sheer force of will, he dragged his gaze toward the church. Strains of music floated through the open doors. People headed inside.

Chloe nudged her fiancé. "We'll save you two a seat."

Maddie tilted her head. "Is everything okay, Tanner?"

He took a breath. "I've never actually been to church before."

Maddie touched his arm. "The natives are friendly here, I promise."

Chloe and Noah made room for them in the pew. Reverend Bryant began the service with a prayer and Tanner followed Maddie's lead. The sermon was thought-provoking.

When the service was over, GeorgeAnne and the rest of her Double Name contingent were welcoming to him. He was taken aback at how many old high school acquaintances with wives and families of their own greeted him.

No one brought up his new coaching job. They all seemed glad to see him, for his sake alone.

Chloe introduced him to Noah's little girl, Lili. With her long, blond pigtails, she was cute. He and Noah made plans to meet at the Jar next week.

Tanner walked Maddie to her car. "Who knew Noah Knightley would be such a likable guy?"

"So are you." She opened the car door. "When you give people a chance to know you." She slipped into the driver's seat.

"Wait." Not yet ready to say goodbye, he held on to the door. "You don't seem your usual self."

"I—I had a lot on my mind last night." Her gaze skittered to a squirrel making an inordinate amount of noise in a nearby oak. "So I made pumpernickel bread."

He rested his arms on the top of the door. "Thinking about your dad?"

Maddie's eyes flew to his and away. "Why do you ask?"

"I was wondering...if you didn't have plans... If you weren't tired of hanging out with me..."

"What, Tanner?"

"Maybe you'd be up for a hike to the waterfall this afternoon? I haven't been there since high school."

Known mainly to locals, the waterfall was off the beaten path in the nearby state forest.

Maddie smiled at him. "How about I slice the pumpernickel and make some pastrami sandwiches? We could combine a picnic lunch with the hike, if that's good with you."

Something in his gut eased. He and Maddie were going to be okay.

He grinned. "Sounds perfect."

"Give me fifteen minutes to go home before we head up the mountain." Tanner grimaced. "I need to mend fences with my mom."

Maddie arched her eyebrow. "What's happened?"

"I shouldn't have pressed her to come to church with me." He closed her car door with a gentle snick. "See you soon."

At her house, she put on a pair of jeans, hiking boots and a puffy black vest over her winter-white wool sweater.

She'd just placed the last of the food in the brown wicker basket when he arrived.

"Great timing." She smiled at him. "How are things with your mother?"

He shook his head. "Mom wouldn't come out of her room."

"I'm sorry."

He shrugged. "It'll blow over. It always does, sooner or later."

For his sake, she hoped it was sooner.

He hefted the basket. "You ready?"

She held the door for him. "Let the adventure begin."

Entering the state forest, the paved road eventually turned into a rutted dirt track. She kept her hold on the basket in the seat between them. Branches whipped at the windshield.

When the washboard road ended, he stopped the truck. "Rest of the way is on foot."

She slipped her arms through the straps of the black backpack with the bottles of water. "Do you remember the trail to the waterfall?"

"Like it was yesterday." His eyes gleamed with anticipation. "I loved that spot. Went there when I needed to get away from the noise."

Not for the first time, she reflected on how troubled—and lonely—his home life must have been.

Toting the basket, he led the way. Reaching the top of the ridge, he paused to take in the view.

"It's spectacular." His breath fogged in the crisp mountain air. "You probably come here all the time." Always the consummate athlete, he hadn't broken a sweat.

"Not so much anymore." Winded, she sucked in a lungful of oxygen. "The downside of being a pastry chef, I guess. My only real cardio is kneading bread."

She motioned toward the range of mountains on the distant horizon. "Peak leaf color won't be for a few weeks."

He smiled. "Then we'll have to come back, won't we?"

It required another ten minutes of strenuous effort to follow the circuitous path over fallen logs and around giant boulders to the base of the gorge.

He cocked his head at the roaring of the waterfall. Exchanging a smile, they pushed through the tangle of laurel and to a small basin which the towering waterfall plunged into. Faint plumes of spray misted her cheeks.

Tanner set the basket at her feet. "Let me check the area for snakes."

Standing by the edge of the pool lapping over the rocks, she shuddered. Snakes were no joke. As the temperatures cooled, rattlesnake activity heated up. Falling leaves provided ideal camouflage.

Grabbing a stick, he brushed aside last year's leaf debris on the forest floor and cleared a flat area, large enough to spread the gray-striped flannel blanket.

After settling onto the blanket, she dispensed the food. After they said grace, he reached for one of the sandwiches. "The hike made me hungry."

"You're always hungry."

His mouth quirked. "True."

After demolishing the contents of the basket,

he lay back and propped his arm behind his head. "Would it bother you if I took a nap?"

"Have at it."

She gathered the remains of their lunch. Mountain kids learned early to tote out what they brought into the natural beauty of the Blue Ridge Mountains.

"You can't imagine how many times over the years I've imagined myself here again," he whispered.

Maddie stilled.

Surrounded by a glade of trees, a small circle of blue Carolina sky hovered above the top of the ridge. It was there his gaze fixed.

"The most beautiful, peaceful place I've ever been. I didn't understand what it was when I was a boy, but I recognize it now." He turned toward her. "Same feeling as at church today. Same feeling I got under the stars on an oil rig when my co-worker told me about faith." He shrugged. "Sounds crazy, doesn't it?"

"Not at all." She eased closer, folding her legs under her. "It's easier to feel God here."

He didn't hear her, though. His eyelids had drifted shut. Living with SandraLynn—with anyone struggling with addiction issues—must be like walking on eggshells. As a boy, there'd always been a tense, hyper-vigilant energy about him.

Maddie regarded it a high compliment that he felt safe enough to fall asleep with her.

She took off her vest and pillowed it under her

neck. She must have drowsed off, too, because she opened her eyes to find him resting on his side, turned toward her. His blue-eyed gaze was enigmatic.

"Oh, hi." She blinked rapidly. "I have a habit of falling asleep on you, don't I?"

"This time it was me who fell asleep first."

She sat up. "You fell asleep before I could get your opinion on a recipe I'm experimenting with for Noah's groom's cake."

"I won't say no to that." He sat up, too. "By the way, I've been meaning to ask you something."

Opening the basket, she rummaged for the container with the cake slices. "What?"

"I'm surprised you're not married, dating or engaged like everyone else we knew in high school."

Dropping her gaze, she scrounged around the bottom of the basket for the utensils she'd placed there.

He was the last person she wanted to share her recent revelation about the reason for her single status.

She passed him the cake. "Why is there no woman in *your* life?"

"I'm content to remain as I am."

Maddie handed him a fork. "You want to be alone for the rest of your life?"

"Seems like more trouble than it's worth, to be honest with you."

"Not every relationship is like your parents' marriage, Tanner."

He stabbed the cake with the fork. "I'm not willing to take that chance."

"You never let anyone fully in, do you?" She sighed. "That's sad. And no way to live. You're going to miss out on so much that's wonderful because of fear."

His mouth thinned. "My mom takes a lot of my emotional energy."

Tanner's mother was needy, but she knew she mustn't say that out loud.

He hunched his shoulders. "I don't have anything left over for anyone else. I'm trying to be a good son. Mom's not had an easy life."

"You're a good son, Tanner."

He shook his head. "My father would disagree."

"Your father is a jerk."

Tanner's gaze snapped up.

"Any man who would abandon his wife and child, especially a wonderful son like you, must be a jerk."

"That's what GeorgeAnne says, too." His gaze softened. "I count myself blessed to be your friend."

Friend. Maddie reckoned she could easily come to hate that word.

Then he twined his fingers through hers. Her heartbeat accelerated. But she tried not to read too much into it.

Men thought differently about such gestures than women. He'd been clear with her—friends only.

"With friendship, like in football, it's probably

best to stick to the rules." She eased her fingers out of his grasp. "No illegal touching."

His brow furrowed. "What do you mean?"

"We've been seen together twice now. At the restaurant last night and at church today."

He scowled. "We've been friends since we were teenagers."

"You really have been away too long if you don't remember how small Southern towns work. How the Truelove grapevine works."

"I still don't know what you mean."

Gathering what was left of their picnic, she repressed the urge to throw something at him. "In the spirit of mutual clarity—you might want to have a word with your matchmaker neighbor."

He frowned. "Clarity?"

"We wouldn't want GeorgeAnne or the rest of the matchmakers to get the wrong idea about our friends-only status." She got off the blanket.

"Where are you going?"

"It's a long climb to the ridge. Once the sun goes behind the mountain, the light goes out like the flicking of a switch."

Grabbing the basket, she left him to bring the blanket and the backpack.

She was nearly to the top when he finally caught up to her.

"I'll carry the basket, Maddie."

They trudged along together in awkward silence until they reached the truck.

She reminded herself he had a lot to deal with

right now. "You'll be fine at school tomorrow, Tanner."

He stowed the basket and the blanket behind the seat. "You are the kindest person I've ever known, Mads."

When it came to him, what she was, was a pushover. Her feelings for him went back a long way and were complicated. For her, their friendship was full of potential emotional land mines. For the sake of her own heart, she needed to take a page from his playbook.

The terms of their friendship would only work if strict guidelines were followed.

Because, as every good baker worth their pastry knew, no one, not even Tanner Price, got to have their cake and eat it, too.

Chapter Eight

Monday morning, Tanner was too nervous to stop by Madeline's. He made do with a piece of toast, but the bread failed to brown or pop up.

His mom tied her bathrobe tighter around her waist. "That toaster hasn't worked for weeks."

Jiggling the lever, he hoped it wasn't an indication of how the rest of his day would turn out. His mother insisted on making his lunch, which was sweet. But it made him feel like a kindergartner headed off for his first day at school.

Even though Coach had first-period planning—which explained his daily cinnamon roll habit—Tanner opted to head into school early to meet with the veteran teacher assigned to mentor him.

Dressed in his trademark suit and bow tie, Mr. Jackson had taught honors English at Truelove High even longer than Maddie's dad had been the football coach. Naturally, with Tanner's former academic record, he'd never been one of the older African American gentleman's students.

"Coach has used the same lesson plans for years."

Mr. Jackson's dark eyes regarded him. "To quote the man himself, 'If it ain't broke, don't fix it.'"

Mr. Jackson stumbled over "ain't" as if it pained him, but his face was kind. "I'll check in with you this afternoon."

Walking into the gym for second period, Tanner had been less scared confronting raging oil fires than facing the thirty-some fourteen-year-olds sitting on the bleachers.

Ninth grade physical education classes were an essential credit per North Carolina graduation requirements. However, the morning went better than he'd expected.

Thanks to his retired jersey in a glass case mounted on the wall in the lobby of the gym, Tanner's reputation as star quarterback of a championship team preceded him. It afforded him enough street cred with the students that he encountered none of the challenges he'd feared a substitute might face. At six foot three, his size provided enough deterrent so that most would think twice before challenging him.

One of the perks of Coach being the athletic director was that Tanner didn't have lunch duties. Instead, he ate in Coach's office and went over his plans for football practice that afternoon.

The last period of the day was the sophomore study hall. Notified of the location change, the students trickled into the classroom next to his—Coach's—office.

Tanner waited for them in front of the whiteboard. Most of the teens claimed seats toward the back. He would have done the same. He was surprised there were only about a dozen students.

Calling out names, he went through the attendance roster. All present and accounted for. This would be his smallest class. Writing *Mr. Price* on the board felt weird. He went over a few rules Mr. Jackson had suggested to maintain order in his classes.

Slouched in their chairs, avoiding eye contact, the group was unnervingly silent.

He wasn't sure why the rookie teacher had been so eager to trade a Civics class for this bunch. They were a motley crew—lots of body piercings, tattoos, etc.—but the kids were absolutely no trouble. They were completely unengaged.

Expecting them to work on homework, he'd been prepared to help as much as his own scholastic abilities allowed. He was better at math and science than subjects that required a lot of reading and writing.

But no one broke out their backpacks. Some had no backpacks at all. Several actually laid their heads on their desks and went to sleep. Though remaining upright, the others appeared in varying states of slumber.

Truelove High had a zero cell phone policy in the classroom. Trying to set a good example, he refrained from taking out his phone.

But he was bored. The kids were bored. Excruciatingly, mind-numbingly bored.

Weren't they supposed to be doing something? He had a hard time doing nothing. What was wrong?

The fifty-minute period felt twice as long by the time the dismissal bell rang. Springing up, the students headed for the door. At the corner of his desk, one of the guys stopped.

The fifteen-year-old's shaggy, dirty-blond hair obscured his eyes. Not that he made eye contact.

When the boy didn't speak, Tanner frowned. "Yes?"

The boy hunched his shoulders. "On Mondays, the other teacher let us clean up the field after Friday's game." The kid was so soft-spoken Tanner had to lean forward to catch his words.

Still no eye contact.

"And you are?"

"Preston, sir." The boy's voice was respectful, if somewhat unsure of himself. "Preston Buckner."

"Why would you want to pick up trash, Preston?"

For the first time, the boy looked at him. His eyes were hazel.

"It gets the grounds ready for the next game." Dropping his gaze, he stuffed his hands in his pockets.

Tanner would far rather be outside than cooped up indoors. Besides, anything to avoid a repeat of today's "study" period.

"Sure, Preston. Tomorrow. We'll do that."

The boy's head snapped up as if he was surprised his request had been granted. "Thanks, Mr. Price."

He shuffled out, joining the throngs making their mass exodus to the buses.

Mr. Jackson found Tanner in his office. "How did it go?"

"Good, except study hall was strange. No one did any studying, much less homework. One student asked if it would be all right if they picked up trash around the school tomorrow. Is that normal?"

"An odd request. Could I see the roster?"

He handed him the attendance book. Scanning the page, Mr. Jackson's eyes narrowed.

"Buckner. Clark. King. Oh, I see." Mr. Jackson returned the record to him. "Truelove High is small. I recognize the names. At some point during the school year, each of them will turn sixteen. Then, like their siblings and parents, they, too, will drop out of school."

His eyebrows rose. "They're waiting to drop out of school?"

Mr. Jackson nodded.

"But why?"

Mr. Jackson sat on the edge of the desk. "They'll drop out because no one in their family has ever graduated from high school. They get no support at home. I suspect, like you, many of them have undiagnosed learning disabilities."

"But the guidance counselor—"

"Does the best she can. Teachers and staff are overworked and underappreciated." Mr. Jackson folded his hands on his lap. "Do you have any idea of the long hours I write college referrals for my students? The strings I pull? The phone calls I make? The other teachers do the same."

"Why isn't something being done for kids like Preston?"

"Those children fell through the cracks of our educational system long ago. They had no one at home to advocate for them."

Just like Tanner until Maddie came into his life.

"They have no special talents like athletics, musical or artistic ability."

He clenched his jaw. "So, what? They don't matter?"

"They do matter, but there are only so many of us. The band director will shepherd those in his fold. The art teachers encourage those within their purview. We are underfunded. It's sad, but no one has ever cared enough to help them through school. Therefore, they will spend their sophomore year biding their time until they're old enough to drop out."

"What happens to them then?"

Mr. Jackson sighed. "Those who don't wander into drugs or crime will get the lowest-paying jobs available. The greatest tragedy is that at fifteen they already know their future is bleak. Worse, they accept it as inevitable."

Was there anything worse than no hope?

His God-given football prowess had given him a chance for something more. It was the very reason he was staying on in Truelove to ensure the guys on the team had their shot. But Preston and the others wouldn't have that.

Outrage began to build in his belly. "This isn't right."

Mr. Jackson peered at him over his eyeglasses. "No, it is not."

All through practice, the conversation with Mr. Jackson bothered Tanner.

Later, with his mom working the closing shift at the pharmacy, he had the house to himself. And more time to brood about the kids in his study hall.

Maddie called him later that night. "How was your first day, Coach Price?"

The smile in her voice boosted his spirits. He leaned his head against the couch cushion and pressed the cell to his ear. "I survived."

"That sounds ominous."

"Actually, it went well. How did it go with Coach's transfer to the acute-care facility?"

"Pretty good." She sighed. "No surprise, he's already made a dozen friends."

"Apples and trees."

She laughed. "You think I talk a lot?"

He smiled into the phone. "It's a gift the way you and your father make people feel valued. I wish I could be more like you."

"And here I'm wishing I could be more like you."

He sat up. "Why would you want to be like me?"

"You're one of the strongest people I know. I love how you aren't afraid to take on any challenge."

"Facing the teenage hordes, I was plenty afraid today."

"But you didn't allow fear to stop you from doing what you felt to be right. Your dogged determination—"

"My hardheadedness, you mean?"

"Your never-quit determination does you credit."

He always felt better after talking to her. "Trust you to see the positive side of my character flaws."

The next morning, he got up in time to make a Madeline's run before school. More than coffee, he needed the lift seeing Maddie provided.

His second day on the job proved much the same as the first. Except, at final period, he took the study group out to the field.

Preston surprised him by organizing the kids into three teams and assigning different areas to collect trash left behind from last Friday's game.

Sitting on the bleachers, elbows on his knees, Tanner observed several things.

Preston had undeveloped leadership skills. The goth girl—or whatever the current lingo was now—had a crush on Preston. A fact to which Preston appeared completely unaware.

Later, back in the classroom before dismissal, Tanner could see everyone felt better from being outdoors and having accomplished something worthwhile. He had a better handle on the individual students in the class. But tomorrow promised a return to mind-numbing boredom for everyone.

They were good kids. Who knew what each of them might be if anyone ever truly invested in them?

From the dull, glazed look in their eyes, he suspected a few had already fallen into harmful practices that provided the illusion their lives mattered. But such roads led to nowhere but addiction, crime, jail and early death.

The wasted potential made him sick to his stomach.

On his way out the door Wednesday morning, he took the toaster with him on a whim.

He'd always been good at taking things apart. Maybe he could fix it. It would give him something to do during study period.

The halls were buzzing with talk of the upcoming apple festival on Saturday. He hadn't been to one of those in years. Perhaps Maddie would go with him.

It was always more fun to go with a friend. Maddie made everything more fun. At least, for him.

That afternoon, five minutes into study period, the kids were already zoned out. He placed the busted toaster and the tools he'd brought on his desk.

Attempting to unscrew the bottom plate of the toaster, he sensed someone hovering. He looked up.

"What're you doing, Mr. Price?"

Preston again.

"It's broken. I thought I'd open it up, take a look and see if I could fix it for my mother."

Skinny shoulders hunched, Preston nodded.

He held the screwdriver out to him. "Would you like to try?"

The boy shied away. "I might break it."

"It's already broke. Give it a try. Nothing to lose."

But Preston just looked at him.

With a hitch in his gut, he suddenly realized this kid couldn't face another failure. "I've never been good at anything but taking things apart and putting them back together."

"That's not true."

He glanced at the overweight girl dressed from head to toe in black. He racked his brain for her name. Leah.

She sniffed. "You were good at football."

"I was good at football, but not enough to make a life out of it."

Suddenly, no one was sleeping anymore.

"I was terrible at school, but everyone's good at something. It's just a matter of finding out what." He pushed the screwdriver across the desk toward Preston. "I'll walk you through it."

He had everyone's attention now. "True failure would've been to stop trying to discover what I might be good at."

Preston picked up the screwdriver.

Tanner rose. "Why don't you sit here?"

Cheeks flushed at the unaccustomed spotlight, Preston sat down. His attempts to use the tools were awkward, but Tanner talked him through it. One by one, the kids drifted closer to get a better look.

Eventually, the guts of the toaster lay spread across the desktop.

Leah propped her hands on her hips. "Now what?"

He bit off a smile. "Now we make a diagnosis."

Someone snickered.

He pointed. "The heating element is usually the first to go. A case of 'they truly don't make 'em like they used to.'"

"Yeah." Another boy—Hudson?—dug his hands into his pockets. "My Nana's toaster is ancient, but it's still going."

Tanner smiled. "While this more modern one—"

"—is junk."

Tanner nodded. "The more features, the greater the chance for something to malfunction." He glanced at the clock on the wall. "Looks like the period is almost over."

"You're not going to leave it like this, are you?" Leah folded her arms over her black leather jacket. "Shouldn't we fix it?"

"If you want to." Too much adult enthusiasm would send them running straight into their shells again.

"The lever's not working, either." He jiggled it to demonstrate. "We could work on that and put it back together tomorrow, I guess."

Hudson shrugged. "Why not?"

A tougher nut to crack, Leah examined her black-painted nails. "Whatever."

The bell rang.

"Bye, Mr. Price," several of them called out.

Lesson plan for tomorrow's study period? To fix what was broken.

After practice, he went to GeorgeAnne's house. She'd run the family hardware store for decades before her sons had taken over.

"You wouldn't happen to know where I could get my hands on any small household appliances that are on the fritz, would you?"

His neighbor surveyed him over the rim of her glasses. "We make it a point to sell our customers working appliances, dear heart."

Tanner laughed. He explained what had happened in class.

She rummaged in a kitchen drawer. Taking out a hammer, she banged the side of the toaster on her kitchen counter.

"Miss GeorgeAnne! What're you doing?"

She handed him the battered toaster. "Consider this my contribution to their future."

GeorgeAnne put in a call to her double-named compatriots, asking for any malfunctioning—or damaged on purpose—counter gadgets. She promised her oldest son, Brian, would deliver the non-working appliances to Tanner tomorrow.

The next day, Preston arrived with a heating element he'd scrounged from an older model toaster at the landfill where his uncle worked.

"No guarantees," the boy warned as his classmates gathered around Tanner's desk.

Leah shot him a fond look. "But the only real loser is a quitter too lazy to try."

Everyone cut their eyes at her.

Her black-painted lips pursed. "It's what my grandma used to say."

Once installed, the new-old heating element did the trick. It was Leah who figured out how to repair the busted pop-up mechanism.

With Tanner's permission, Hudson took the hall pass to beg a loaf of bread from his aunt, who worked in the cafeteria. When he returned with bread and a tub of butter, Tanner let them take turns toasting the bread. Everyone had a slice.

GeorgeAnne's son, Brian Allen, walked in just then. "Y'all starting a repair club?"

Tanner hadn't thought of it that way. "Maybe?"

Preston took the box from Brian. "Whatcha got there, Mr. Allen?"

Bless him, Brian had included small toolkits. Enough for each group of three. He also stayed the rest of the period to help.

Later at the Jar for team-building night, GeorgeAnne set a plate of lasagna in front of him. "Brian told me about the difference you've already made for those kids."

Maddie placed this week's dessert next to his glass. "What's this?"

Coconut cake. A Southern autumn specialty.

"It was nothing much." He rubbed his neck. "Just trying to pass the time. They seem to have gotten into it."

"Nonsense," GeorgeAnne tutted. "Tanner has

a real gift with the kids." She walked away to harangue one of the ROMEOs.

Maddie sank into the chair beside him. "Why didn't you tell me?"

It had been a busy week for him. For the bakery, too.

Shrugging, he stuck his fork into the lasagna.

"I want all the details."

"Show me around the apple festival this weekend, and I'll tell you about it."

Maddie extended her hand. "Deal." Her hand felt soft and warm in his. "Another football win to look forward to Friday night and the festival."

"I like your confidence."

She nudged his shoulder. "I believe in you, Tanner."

Because she had faith in him, it was easier to have faith in himself.

Kind of like what was happening with the study hall kids?

By the end of the school day on Friday, the kids had somehow managed to repair every small kitchen appliance Brian Allen had brought over.

He surveyed their handiwork. "Job well done, ladies and gentlemen."

Leah rolled her eyes, but he could tell she was pleased with herself, too.

Preston beamed at him. "What now, Mr. Price?"

When was the last time these students had experienced any success at school?

The Double Name Club had managed to wrangle

a device from nearly everyone in Truelove. Possibly even the tri-county area. But what now, indeed?

These kids couldn't afford to lose their newfound momentum.

Then he had an idea.

That night, Truelove won the away game.

Due to the festival, Madeline's was packed on Saturday morning. The square was crowded with Truelove citizens and vendors selling all types of handicrafts. But because of her new part-time helpers, Maddie was able to meet him around noon.

"I saved you a chocolate croissant."

Tanner grinned. "Thanks for thinking of me."

She threw him an interesting look, but she didn't comment. He was having a harder and harder time not thinking of her all the time.

They drove to Apple Valley Orchard. She bought a bushel of apples from Callie McAbee. Jake McAbee and his children, Maisie and Micah, took them on a hayride through the apple trees with his tractor.

Returning to his truck, Tanner hesitated before cranking the engine. "Do you need to get back right away?"

"No." She tilted her head. "What are you thinking?"

"I need to make a run to the big-box store on the highway. I've had this idea for a new class project for the study-period kids. I'll also need to stop by the Burger Barn."

"Hungry already?"

"No, but for this plan to work it might be wise to show up with a few incentives."

"Fascinating... Count me in."

He chewed his lip. "It will either be a big hit with them, or it may tank any credibility I've managed to build."

"I'm game. Let's go."

Leaving the orchard behind, he headed in the direction of the highway. They passed the church.

"Mind if I join you at church again?"

Across the truck cab, she smiled at him. "You're always welcome."

"This week, I've thought a lot about Reverend Bryant's sermon."

"Pastor Bryant and my dad are good friends. He's a great guy, and a real blessing to our community. Especially when you consider what he had to overcome..." Biting her lip, she turned toward the window.

"What do you mean?"

"Forget it." She waved her hand. "I shouldn't have said anything."

"What, Maddie?"

Cheeks flushed, she continued to stare out the window at the countryside rolling past. "His father was an abusive drunk. His mother raised him by herself."

What she hadn't said ticked between them for a few seconds. That the reverend's childhood hadn't been so different from his.

"If you ever need someone to talk to, Pastor Bryant would understand, Tanner."

He stiffened.

"Are you mad at me?" Her voice had gone small.

"No." He looked at her. Her eyes bored into his. "I realize it's coming from a place of concern. But I'm not a guy who likes to talk about his feelings."

"Maybe you'd feel better if you did."

She might be right, but it wasn't his way.

"I prefer to not talk about my family anymore." He steered the truck onto the highway. "Besides, I'll need your help in the toy store."

Her mouth twitched. "Okay, now you've really got me intrigued."

Tanner hoped Preston and company would agree.

In the toy store, Maddie tossed him one of those soft footballs.

Easily catching it, he grinned. "Not bad for a pastry chef. Coach would be proud."

She laughed. "Like you said, apples and trees."

The next day, on Monday morning, he decided to run his idea past Mr. Jackson.

"I give you full points for thinking outside the box with this crowd, Mr. Price." The straitlaced, by-the-book, old-school gentleman steepled his hands under his chin. "Kudos to you for trying. I hope it works."

That afternoon, Tanner faced the study-period kids. He'd taken the time Sunday afternoon to examine a few of their records. Several of them had birthdays early in the year, including Preston.

He didn't have long to get them invested in their own education. Tanner couldn't stand losing any of them.

"I have a new project for us to tackle."

Leah's eyes narrowed. "Why are there buckets of plastic toys on our desks?"

"I'm glad you asked, Miss King." He held up a tiny red bricklike square. He connected it to a blue one. "You will note how they interlock."

Hudson snickered. "It's a LEGO, dude."

"It's a building block, Mr. Clark. And with it, we can build anything." He scanned their faces. "Each of you must build something with the bucket of blocks on your desk."

"We're not children, Mr. Price," Leah growled.

Adolescents were notoriously touchy about being perceived as grown-up. He remembered what it was like to be fifteen and wanting to be an adult. Yet, he knew adulthood wasn't all it was cracked up to be.

"You will be judged on creativity, execution and functionality."

Preston's eyes widened. "You mean you want us to make our creatures do something?"

He bit back a smile. "Creations, Mr. Buckner. Not creatures—but yes. And to sweeten things—"

Tanner fanned the cards he'd bought. "You will also receive a gift card to the Burger Barn."

Leah's forehead furrowed. "For playing with a bunch of toys?"

"For completing the assigned project, yes."

Hudson's hand shot in the air. "I'm in."

Preston grinned. "Cool, Mr. Price."

As if she couldn't have cared less, Leah studied the cuticle beneath her black-painted thumbnail. "How much time do we have?"

Gotcha.

First, he made them sketch out their ideas onto graph paper. After spending another day fine-tuning their drawings, using one of the programs in Ms. Markham's computer lab, he helped them transfer their designs into computer-generated blueprints.

Once the construction phase began, he made a second run to the toy store. He'd underestimated not only their ingenuity but also how many blocks twelve high school students would need.

Ten days later, as the September calendar flowed into October, they submitted their creations for review. He recruited Mr. Jackson, Ms. Markham, a physics teacher and the art teacher to help him judge the projects. They awarded prizes for Most Creative, Best Use of Color, Most Likely to Take Over the World, etc.... The projects were amazing. He was so proud of the students he could almost burst.

Mr. Jackson shook his hand. "Congratulations, Coach Price, on a well-executed lesson plan."

Tanner felt like he'd received the equivalent of a Nobel Prize.

"What do you have planned for the rest of the semester?"

Tanner scrubbed his forehead. "Hadn't gotten that far yet."

"Have you ever heard of the National Robotics Competition?"

Tanner shook his head.

"It combines the excitement of sport with the rigor of technology. A high school team must work together to build an industrial-size robot. Rising through district, state and regional competitions, they might eventually compete against robotics teams from across the country."

"Might?" He jutted his chin. "I assure you this crew would definitely make it to nationals."

The English teacher gave him that thin little smile of his. "Based on what I've seen here today, the kids might find it cool."

A kernel of excitement began to build inside him. "It would give them a reason to not drop out."

"Come by my office tomorrow, and we'll go over the details."

Maddie walked into the classroom with a platter of cupcakes. Surrounding her, the students immediately claimed one for themselves. Tanner was doubly proud when they each thanked her.

Watching them inspect the projects displayed around the room, he and Maddie hung out near the whiteboard.

"You didn't have to bring cupcakes, Maddie, but thank you."

She smiled. "Success should be celebrated."

"They would've been thrilled with whatever was left in your display case."

"Absolutely not!" She looked at him like he'd grown two heads. "Nothing but the best for your kids."

They *were* his kids. All of them. The football team and the kids no one but him believed in.

When had this become the hardest job he'd ever loved?

Chapter Nine

It wasn't even the holiday rush yet, but over the next few weeks, Maddie was run ragged at the bakery.

She'd made lots of petit fours for the baby showers And a cute, totally fun Gotcha cake for little Finn when he was adopted by Jack and Kate Dolan at the equestrian center.

Maddie made the deliveries herself. She fell into bed exhausted. There wasn't enough hours in the day for all that needed to be done.

And of course, she was angst-ing big-time over the cake for Chloe's upcoming wedding.

Noah had told her to spare no expense in making it the cake of Chloe's dreams.

Saturday morning, after the shop closed, she wondered if perhaps she'd finally gone beyond the reach of her talent.

It was an elaborate, beautiful cake. But how in the world was she going to get the multiple layers to the wedding venue?

She was carefully placing the fourth tier on top of the third when the supports gave way. The cake teetered. Maddie made a wild grab to keep it off the floor.

Tanner chose that moment to arrive. "Whoa." He rushed forward to help. "What happened?"

She burst into tears. "It's a disaster. I've ruined Chloe's wedding. I should've never tried to have this many tiers."

"Let's set this on the counter and take a minute to evaluate what we can do to fix this situation."

He helped her put it down.

"There is no fixing it," she sobbed. "Why did I ever think I could make someone's wedding cake?"

"Your cakes are wonderful." Hand on his chin, he circled the cake. "I think what we have here isn't so much a baking issue as an engineering dilemma."

She sniffed. "What do you mean?"

"Have you got any icing left?"

Gulping past the boulder in her throat, she nodded.

"The tiers just need more support. Got any more of those dowel rods?"

She made a dash for the supply closet. While she repaired the icing damage, Tanner figured out a more secure system of fastening the tiers to each other.

Forgetting about their friend pact, she was so grateful she hugged him. Hard.

At his startled look, she blushed and let go. "Sorry."

His face wore an expression she wasn't sure how to decipher.

Turning toward the cake, she clasped her hands under her chin. "You're a genius, Tanner Price."

"Hardly." He shrugged, but his mouth curved. "Glad to be of service."

"Now I've got to get it to the reception without demolishing it again." She rubbed her forehead. "I've never made anything so colossal before."

"It had to be colossal. Chloe's invited most of the town, right?"

Tanner was going as Maddie's plus-one.

A friends-only plus-one.

"We're going to have to take it apart again. Box it up and reassemble it on-site."

She groaned.

"We know what to do now." He grinned. "It'll be a piece of cake."

They went out to the alley to examine the space in her car.

He scratched his head. "How do you make deliveries in the Beetle?"

"It's not easy." She sighed. "But I've never had an order of this magnitude before. One day I hope to purchase a van customized for deliveries."

He closed the trunk. "Next week, I'll install some compartments to make it easier for you, but for now, how about we take my truck?"

They transferred the individual layers to his vehicle out front. Tanner drove cautiously down Main Street, across the bridge and past the Welcome to

Truelove sign. Her job was to keep the boxes from sliding. She also kept an anxious eye on the clock.

"There were a lot of deliveries this morning. We're going to be late."

"We won't be late," he reassured her.

She was a nervous wreck by the time they reached the venue at the top of the mountain.

Despite running behind schedule, with Tanner's help, she managed to put the tiers together without further mishap.

He wiped his brow. "Teaching ninth graders isn't as stressful as delivering this cake. Maybe you should consider hiring someone else to make deliveries."

"Not a bad idea." She cocked her head, surveying the cake for any problem areas. "It would have to be someone super-conscientious, reliable—"

"—with wicked engineering skills?" He laughed.

Cake crisis averted, they headed for the dressing rooms to change into their party clothes. They met up at the French doors and paused on the terrace overlooking the flower-bedecked stone gazebo below. Rows of white chairs lined the grassy area. People had started arriving and taking their seats.

It was a glorious day. She was so happy for Chloe. She prayed the day would be everything her friend hoped for and more.

For the first time, she was able to take stock of Tanner's wedding attire. The navy-blue suit brought out the green in his eyes.

"Wow, you clean up nice, Coach."

He smiled. "You don't look so bad yourself."

She gave him a mock curtsy. "Thank you, kind sir, for the compliment."

Maddie didn't think she'd ever be as gorgeous as someone like Kelsey McKendry, who ran the wedding venue. But today, she knew she looked good in the burgundy chiffon tea-length dress and high heels.

A breeze blew a tendril of hair across her cheek. Before she could brush it away, his hand caught the curl between his fingers.

"Silky, like I thought," he murmured before tucking it behind her ear.

"One of these days, I'm going to cut it short."

His brow creased. "Don't."

She gazed into those inscrutable eyes of his. "Okay," she rasped.

All of a sudden, her knees felt wobbly.

He took a breath and offered his arm. "Shall we?"

But there was no chance anyone would mistake them for a couple. Over the last few weeks, he'd made it clear—sometimes embarrassingly clear—to everyone that was all they were: friends.

Kind of like what she was with Zach. Except her feelings for the town mechanic were nothing like what she felt for Tanner.

The wedding went off without a hitch. Chloe was so beautiful she glowed with her love for Noah. And the couple was delighted with the wedding cake.

Tanner nudged her. "Another cake in the *Win* column."

"Delivery took five years off my life, though."

He tilted his head. "I've just had another idea."

Maddie's mouth quirked. "Should I be afraid?"

"You've met Preston."

Nodding, she watched Noah lead Chloe out onto the parquet floor for their first dance. Tanner kept her updated on the robotic crew's progress.

"Conscientious. Reliable." He ticked the qualities off on his fingers. "Wicked engineering skills."

"And?"

He cocked his head. "What about hiring Preston to do deliveries for you after school and on weekends? He's got his driver's license now."

"And he's still in school. He didn't drop out."

Tanner smiled. "His uncle gave him an old jalopy. They've got it working again. He and I could install that shelf system I was telling you about earlier."

She raised an eyebrow. "It's fixed up enough to carry one of my cakes?"

"It will be pristine, I promise you, by the time he delivers your first cake. He's got unbelievable fine motor skills. With training, Preston might even be able to work the storefront and wield a pastry bag, too."

She looked at him. "You never give up on those kids, do you?"

Uncomfortable with praise, he shrugged. "Your

father never gave up on me. I won't give up on them."

She looked at him.

He frowned. "What?"

Tanner Price didn't grasp what a special person he was, and she'd only make him defensive if she tried to tell him.

"Tell Preston to come talk to me after school on Monday. Three o'clock sharp."

He smiled. "Thanks, Mads, for investing in him."

She bit off a sigh. Preston Buckner wasn't the only one she was invested in.

Tanner loosened his tie. "The job would be contingent on him staying in school, of course."

"It won't be the robot or the job that keeps Preston in school."

He gave her a perplexed look.

"It will be you, Tanner Price. He'll stay in school because of you."

Like her dad, the word *quit* wasn't in her vocabulary.

Maybe, just maybe, she could convince Tanner to stay in Truelove for reasons that had nothing to do with football.

The regular October football season rolled into November. Each day, he settled a little more into his new role as coach. Each week, the team added another victory in the *Win* column.

What he'd always viewed as a deficit—his dyslexia—had proven to be an asset in coaching. It allowed him a unique perspective to put together creative game strategies that led the team to one victory after another as the season progressed.

He continued to boycott the school cafeteria in favor of lunch at the Mason Jar. Usually with Noah. What started out as a friendly get-together had evolved into a gathering of new friends. Colton Atkinson of Drake Construction. Rancher Clay McKendry. Nate Crenshaw also occasionally dropped in to shoot the breeze with them.

In early November, at the last game before the postseason playoff rounds, the Bobcats' winning streak came to a screeching halt.

The team had been riding a euphoric high ever since the beginning of the season. But over the last couple of practices, they'd slacked off from giving it their all.

Unlike the guys, Tanner wasn't surprised by the defeat. He'd seen it coming. He'd known after the first play that Truelove was going to lose.

Not because their opponent was better, but because the Bobcats didn't want it enough.

On the bus ride back to Truelove, he confronted the shocked and angry teens. "You'll be spending your Saturday going over what you did wrong and reviewing game tape for next week's game so we don't make the same mistakes again."

Kyle groaned. An undercurrent of discontent rumbled through the bus.

"We were robbed," DaShonte muttered.

"No," Tanner said, scowling at them. "You got cocky."

Hurley was the first to drop his head. "Yes, sir."

Tanner looked at each of them. "Nobody's entitled to a state championship. You have to earn it."

Eyes downcast, Javier nodded. "I hear you."

"As for the rest of you, you can check any delusions of grandeur about coasting the rest of the season at the door of this bus." He jabbed his finger at them. "You're not that good, gentlemen. Nobody owes you anything."

DaShonte swallowed hard. "Yes, sir."

"If you want to be state champions, you're going to have to work for it. And work harder than you've ever worked in your life."

"We'll work, Coach." Randall looked around at his teammates. "I promise we won't disappoint you next time."

A lump grew in his throat. It was the first time anyone on the team had called him Coach.

The feeling was strangely satisfying.

It was late by the time he reached the house. His mom had already turned in for the night. The team was in for a punishing workout the next morning. A Saturday practice meant he had to cancel his plans with Maddie.

He texted her the bad news. Seconds later, his cell phone rang.

"Shouldn't you be in bed already?"

"Not until I tell you how sorry I am for tonight's loss."

Something eased in his heart. Hearing her voice had that effect on him. Settling against the cushion, he blew out a slow breath. "They didn't deserve to win. So I lit a fire under them."

He told her what he'd said. "Do you think I was too harsh?"

"Do *you* think you were too harsh?"

He ran his hand over his head. "It paled in comparison to some of your father's ear-blistering tirades back in the day."

"Did it work?"

He smiled into the phone. "We won the state championship that year, didn't we?"

"Exactly. High personal standards coupled with high personal investment in each individual student is my dad's go-to philosophy."

"As Mr. Jackson would say, 'If it ain't broke, then…'"

Maddie snorted. "Mr. Jackson has never said 'ain't' in his life."

"He was quoting your father."

"Ah." Maddie chuckled. "That explains it. You're kind of loving this gig, huh?"

"Let's just say it's growing on me."

"You can lower the drawbridge now, Coach Price. You're among friends."

He grinned. "Fine. I don't hate it."

"I saw Preston at the game tonight."

"How's he doing making deliveries?"

"Preston is a marvel of ingenuity."

Tanner smiled.

"Leah King was at the game, too. She's got a crush on Preston."

"I know. He doesn't." Tanner smirked.

"Typical male."

"On the maturity scale, we men do tend to catch a clue later than the women." He chuckled. "I figure at this point, you and I are finally on an equal playing field."

She sniffed. "You'd think so, wouldn't you?"

He laughed so loud he was afraid he'd woken his mother down the hall. Soon after, they got off the phone.

Maddie was the best friend he'd ever had. Was that all that she was to him, though?

Perhaps if he told himself that often enough, he'd believe it.

Chapter Ten

Last year, the day before Thanksgiving had been the bakery's biggest sales day. Hopefully, Madeline's second annual pie sale would prove to be the same.

At seven on the dot, Ann Randolph prepared to open the door and welcome their first customer of the holiday season. "I hope you've made enough pies."

Unloading a tray of gingerbread into the display case, Maddie rose. "I increased my output by ten percent. I hope I didn't overestimate demand. I hate having product go to waste."

Ann flipped the sign from *Closed* to *Open*. "Somehow I don't think that is going to be a problem."

Dusting off her hands, Maddie joined Ann at the front of the store. She gasped. The line for Madeline's was around the block. "For the love of a croissant..."

"Pies and pastry, too, I imagine." Ann chuckled. "Ready?"

The early-morning hours were a blur. At nine o'clock, Kara arrived and insisted on helping.

Maddie shook her head. "Why aren't you lying in a recliner with your feet propped?"

"Isn't your due date tomorrow?" Ann removed a pie from the case. "Does your family know you're here?"

"I've driven them crazy with my nesting. They're probably glad for a break." Kara gestured toward the stack of orders beside the cash register. "I could ring up patrons while you box the orders."

"Nobody's got time to help you birth a baby in this pastry shop." Maddie wagged her finger at the mom-to-be. "Not to mention what that would do to my health rating."

"No babies will be born today on these premises, I promise."

Ann smirked. "I think it's sweet—if a tad naive—you still think you have any control over when this precious child decides it's time to be born."

Kara sighed. "Please, ladies. Let me help."

Ann shrugged. "We are swamped right now."

Maddie exhaled. "Okay, but you have to stay off your feet and sit on this stool the entire time."

Kara nodded. "Absolutely. I will not get off this stool."

Maddie wasn't sure how they would have managed without her. Pumpkin, apple and sweet potato pies were the usual bestsellers. She sold out of pecan pie, too.

By one o'clock, she'd emptied the display cases. She locked the door behind the last customer. She swiped her arm across her forehead. "What a day!"

Kara beamed at them. "Well done, ladies."

She sank into a chair. "Thank you, Kara and Ann. I'm not sure how I did this by myself last year."

Kara eased off the stool. "I think next year you should promote preorders. So you can get ahead of the rush." She put her hand atop her belly.

Ann placed her hand on Kara's arm. "Are you feeling okay, hon?"

"Just tired. A good tired."

Maddie stacked the chair on top of the table, as she prepared to mop the floor. "I can put the bakery to rights by myself."

Kara shook her head. "Never refuse free help."

Ann nodded. "Many hands make light work."

Less than an hour later, with the bakery spic and span, Maddie hurried to her car. This weekend, Judy Moore was away visiting family, but she'd asked Tanner and his mom to join them all for Thanksgiving.

Standing beside her car, she took a deep breath of crisp, cold air. Downtown Truelove had a slightly deserted feel that would quickly change come Saturday with the Christmas Parade and Santa on the Square.

On the other side of the river that wended like a horseshoe around the small hamlet, snow rested like a mantle upon the mountains.

Truelove hadn't seen any snow yet. But snow in the valley couldn't be too far behind. Just as long as a snowstorm didn't disrupt the fourth-round playoff game tomorrow night.

Rolling her eyes, she got into her car. *Dad, get out of my head.* She wasn't a football coach's daughter for nothing. And Tanner would have echoed her concerns about the playoffs.

Did she want Tanner out of her head, too? Yes. Out of her heart? Not so much.

Back at the house, she found her father desperate to do something other than rest. "I can help you cook."

"You don't know how to cook, Dad."

He folded his arms across his chest. "My steaks are the stuff of legend."

"In your own mind, perhaps."

"What was that, missy?" Grabbing her around the waist, he pulled her into a bear hug.

She shrieked. "Dad!"

He'd been giving her bear hugs since she was little. He grinned at her. They'd come too close to never sharing another father-daughter moment again.

Tears sprang into her eyes.

"None of that now," he grunted. "I demand you put my skills to use, young lady."

"Your skills only extend as far as a grill."

He pursed his lips. "What would you say to frying the turkey this year?"

She hung up her coat. "In what?"

"I could jerry-rig something." He gave a slow nod. "You'd be free to concentrate on the fixins'."

She shook her head. "You struggle to change the air filters in the house."

"Tanner could definitely rig up something."

She had no doubt Tanner could make it work. "That doesn't exactly inspire confidence, Dad."

"Put your old man and Tanner into the turkey game, Chef." He dropped his head onto her shoulder. "Please. Say yes."

"You are the most ridiculous father ever." She laughed. "But I love you anyway. So yes, you and Tanner—"

"Yahoo!" He pulled out his cell. "We won't let you down." Phone pressed to his ear, he walked into the living room.

That afternoon before Thanksgiving Day, she allowed her dad to take charge of baking the ham. Under her supervision, he basted the ham and stuck in a bunch of whole cloves, arranged in a pattern highly reminiscent of the grid on a football field.

She got out her mother's Thanksgiving decorations—the ones she used every year—and decorated the house. Standing back, she admired the overall effect.

What would Tanner's mom think? Was it too much? Had she tried too hard?

She was anxious—and excited—to share the day with Tanner and get to know his mother.

A certain choreography would need to happen to

put everything on the table warm at the same time. As with life, timing was everything.

In high school, the timing had been wrong for her and Tanner. Was this their second chance? Would now prove to be God's timing for them?

Had she misinterpreted Tanner's interest? He was nothing if not the master of mixed signals. They'd been spending so much time together lately. Surely she wasn't mistaken about his desire to remain in Truelove and see whatever this was between them led?

Could it lead to something wonderful? Or was she merely projecting her feelings onto him?

When her phone dinged, she almost jumped out of her skin. It was Tanner. It took a sec for her heartbeat to stop thudding.

She fought to inject a casual, totally cool, just hanging out, not obsessing about you vibe into her voice. "Oh, Tanner. How are you? What's up?"

The beat of silence stretched long.

"Are you okay, Maddie? Is everything all right?"

Leaning her elbows on the kitchen countertop, she blushed. "Of course, I'm okay. What could be wrong? Why do you ask?"

"Uh… You sound funny. Not your usual self."

She dared not ask what her usual self sounded like—lest he tell her. And shatter any remaining vestiges of self-confidence she possessed.

Was he calling to cancel on her for tomorrow?

Her stomach tanked. She squeezed her eyelids

shut. All that food... Her father would be so disappointed. She would be devastated.

"I understand," she rasped. "Sometimes things can't be helped. Thank you for letting me know."

This was what came from getting her hopes up. She was such a dreamer. And what had that ever brought her but—

"What are you talking about, Maddie? Are you even listening to me?"

"Sorry, would you repeat what you just said, please?"

"I said my mom has gotten it into her head she needs to bring her candied yams as a contribution. I know this is last minute—"

"Your mother wants to bring a dish to Thanksgiving?" Maddie frowned. "You're still coming to my house for dinner?"

"Well, yeah."

She pictured him—brow furrowed in his usual Tanner-esque scowl.

"Mom and I have been looking forward to celebrating Thanksgiving with you and your dad. Why would you think we would cancel?"

Because she was ridiculously insecure and hopelessly invested in making the holiday an event Tanner wouldn't want to walk away from. She needed to chill.

"Mom wants to make a good impression on you and your dad."

She could relate because she had been trying equally hard to impress them.

"I would love for your mom to bring candied yams. One less dish for me to juggle in the lineup going into the oven."

"Glad to hear you've got a game day strategy." He laughed. "Football is in your blood."

"Don't remind me."

"I should let you go. Your father's probably wanting dinner."

She sniffed. "After all the cooking I've done today, he knows better than to expect anything beyond leftovers, cereal or a sandwich."

"I can't wait to celebrate Thanksgiving with you tomorrow."

"Me, too," she breathed.

Clicking off, she was on cloud nine until she felt compelled to put the brakes on her enthusiasm. He probably meant he was looking forward to the food.

That night, she fell asleep thinking about him. Bounding out of bed the next morning, she drew aside the curtain, half afraid the weather had turned gray and drizzly. But there was not a cloud in sight.

She prayed there'd be only blue skies moving forward for her and Tanner.

Tanner got up early to make sure his mother's recipe went off without a hitch. His mom was already in the kitchen at the stove, stirring a wooden spoon in a pot.

Her eyes were clear and bright. "Happy Thanksgiving, honey."

Another bit of tension he hadn't realized was

there leaked away. "I see you've made a start on the candied yams."

The sweet potatoes were nestled in the baking dish, awaiting the sauce she stirred on the stovetop.

He inhaled the intoxicating blend of butter, brown sugar and vanilla wafting from the pot. "Smells wonderful."

Tanner had vague memories of his mother making this recipe for Thanksgiving when he was a boy. "What can I do to help?"

His mom poured the sauce over the sweet potatoes. "Could you open the oven door so I can pop this inside?"

"Sure thing."

His mother inserted the pan on the middle oven rack, closed the door and set the timer. Hands on her bony hips, she surveyed the results of her handiwork. "I think it's turned out all right."

Tanner placed his arm across her shoulders. "It'll be like dessert."

She was in such a better place. And he was so thankful to have his mother back. "It's going to be a wonderful day."

"Every day is wonderful when you're here with me, Tan-Tan."

His chest pinched. A shadow fell over him. Was her sobriety inextricably tied to him? Lasting recovery had to center around the patient's own determination to be well and not around external circumstances or resting upon someone else.

Did her continued welfare depend entirely upon

him? He couldn't stay in Truelove—with her—forever.

Could he? Should he? Shouldn't she want to eventually forge a future for herself? Wasn't that more emotionally healthy? Or was he merely a terrible son?

She smoothed her hand over her dress. "Do you think I look okay?"

Tanner scrubbed his forehead. "You look fantastic, Mom."

His mother gave him a wobbly smile. "It's silly to be nervous. But I am."

This was a big deal for his mom. It was her first social outing in more years than he cared to recall. *God, please let today be a success for her.*

He changed into a white long-sleeved, button-down Oxford shirt and charcoal slacks. Truelove wasn't a formal kind of town, but Thanksgiving with the Lovetts demanded something more than jeans.

Frost still covered the ground when they arrived at Maddie's house. Coach's broad face broke into a welcoming grin as he opened their front door. "Well, if it isn't SandraLynn, the prettiest girl who ever graced Truelove High."

His mother swatted at his arm. "And you're still the biggest flirt this side of the Appalachians."

Tanner got a glimpse of the young woman she'd been. And who she might yet be again.

Coach ushered them through to the kitchen. "Maddie! The Prices are here."

Tanner's heart slammed against his rib cage.

"Miss SandraLynn." Maddie's dark gaze flicked to his and then away. "We are so happy you could join us for Thanksgiving."

Hurrying forward, Maddie hugged his mother. "I love your dress."

"Why, thank you, sweetheart." His mother threw Maddie a shy smile. "You look a right treat yourself." She elbowed Tanner, startling him out of the bemused reverie into which he'd fallen. "Doesn't she, Tanner?"

"Uh, yes, ma'am. Yes, she does."

He had never been the most articulate person, but as usual, when he needed them most, words failed him.

Coach winked at him. "I figured the pilgrim dress of hers is appropriate."

The long-sleeved black dress had a white collar and white cuffs.

His mother wagged her finger at Coach. "Your daughter is lovely. She does not look like a pilgrim. Does she, Tanner?"

"Ummm... No, ma'am." He winced.

"However will I keep my head from swelling at such high praise?" Maddie's dark eyes twinkled. "That's for me, I presume?"

She nudged her chin at the baking dish he'd carried in for his mom.

Coach rubbed his hands together. "Did you bring the fryer contraption, son?"

Maddie made a face. "Not inspiring confidence, Dad."

Tanner grinned. "I consulted an expert and bought only the highest-quality materials."

Coach elbowed his daughter. "I told you Tanner could handle this."

"After talking it over with GeorgeAnne's son, Brian, I bought a deep-fat fryer at their hardware store."

Coach nodded. "Works for me."

"The fryer's in the truck. Where should I set it up?"

Coach put on his football jacket. "On the patio."

"Please be careful, guys. Let's keep this Thanksgiving free from trips to the ER," Maddie teased. "Or should I put the fire department on speed dial?"

Coach put his hand over his heart. "Your lack of confidence in our abilities cuts me to the quick."

She rolled her eyes. "Miss SandraLynn and I will get everything else ready."

It wasn't long before Tanner brought the finished product inside with a beaming Coach at his side.

Maddie smiled. "You actually pulled it off."

"Oh ye of little faith." Her father got out an electric carving knife and plated the turkey. "ETA on meal kickoff?"

She peered at the oven. "Soon as the biscuits are ready."

Coach picked up the turkey platter. "Would you grab the tea pitcher, SandraLynn?" He and Tanner's mom headed to the dining room.

Tanner was pleased to see how at ease his mother appeared. But suddenly he became aware he and Maddie were alone in the kitchen. It was ridiculous to feel so tongue-tied. With Maddie, of all people. They'd just seen each other yesterday.

He needed to say something... Anything...

"You don't look like a pilgrim," he blurted. "You look beautiful."

Blushing, she touched a hand to her hair—that glorious dark mass of curls that fell to her shoulders. "You don't clean up so bad yourself, either."

He realized abruptly how much he loved her hair. Since when did he love anyone's hair?

Without him noticing, he had moved closer to her. Delicious aromas of vanilla, cinnamon and nutmeg teased at his nostrils. Short-circuiting his common sense.

He took a deliberate step backward. "Can I take the biscuits out for you?" He willed his heart to settle.

If she took note of his emotional about-face, she said nothing about it. She handed him two oven mitts. "Be my guest."

Everything was ready at the same time, and he helped her carry all the dishes into the dining room.

Coach was keeping his mom entertained with a highly embroidered tale of Tanner's former derring-do on the football field. In the candlelight, his mother's face had a happy, healthy glow.

"Maddie, you've gone all out." His gaze flicked

between the food to the candles to the autumn decor. "Thank you."

Coach said a blessing. "Amen. Let's eat." He grinned at Tanner. "Don't want to miss kickoff at twelve thirty."

"Just once, Dad, could we give watching football on Thanksgiving Day a pass?"

"It's a tradition, Maddie girl. And this year I've finally got someone watching with me who will appreciate it like I do."

Sitting at the other end of the table, Maddie crossed her arms. "And what about Miss SandraLynn?"

His mother's lips twitched. "As a football mom, I'm used to it."

Tanner shifted in his chair. "Before we watch the game, Coach, it's only fair we do the dishes."

Maddie grinned at him. "And they say chivalry is dead."

After lunch, the men were on cleanup duty. Later, watching the televised collegiate game in the living room, he was amazed to find his mother discussing the finer points of the game with Coach.

"I didn't realize you knew that much about football, Mom."

"You'd be surprised what a mother learns about a topic when her child shows an aptitude."

When Maddie excused herself to put the pies in the oven, he followed her into the kitchen. There was a funny look on her face.

He cocked his head. "What is it?"

She shrugged. "Would you mind doing me a favor?"

"Anything. Name it."

"Careful," she teased. "You don't know what you're signing up for."

"What do you need help with, Mads?"

"Since my dad is a professional football fanatic, we decorate the house for Christmas on Thanksgiving since on Friday he's usually tied up with playoffs. But I don't want him lifting and carrying the boxes out of the attic."

He got off the stool. "I'm your guy." He flushed, realizing how that might come across. "I mean... I'm on it."

Up in the attic, she pointed to several large cardboard cartons. "If you wouldn't mind toting those downstairs."

He carried a stack of two and left her the smaller one to carry.

"When do you and your mom decorate?"

He made sure to duck his head to avoid hitting a low ceiling beam. "We don't. Not since my dad..." He concentrated on not losing his footing on the stairs.

She came to an abrupt halt. "Sorry, I didn't mean to stir up old wounds."

"You didn't." He leaned against the wall in the stairwell. "I've made it a point to get Mom out of the house each year by meeting me wherever I'm working a job. With no permanent residence, I haven't bothered to decorate."

"That sounds lonely."

Why now was he only just realizing it? Not only for him but for his mom.

Maddie tucked a curl behind her ear. "If this is a bad idea, I can do this another day."

"Actually, I think my mom would enjoy decorating your house for Christmas."

He and Maddie unboxed the artificial Christmas tree next to the fireplace in the den. At halftime, he and Coach set out electric candles in the windows while his mom and Maddie decorated the tree.

At the close of the game, Coach handed him a Moravian star.

Using a small step stool, he positioned it on the topmost branch and followed his mother's instructions to tweak it a little left or a smidgeon right.

"Perfection," his mother finally declared.

Coach plugged in the lights and the tree sprang to life. He high-fived Tanner. "Teamwork. That's what I'm talking 'bout."

Maddie fingered her chin. "There's still the outside to decorate—but first let me put the pies in the oven."

Coach glanced at his watch. "The next game starts at four thirty."

"Dad!" she groaned, and gave him strict instructions to summon her when the timer went off.

Tanner strung the lights along the eaves of the roof for a cheery gingerbread-house vibe.

"Appropriate." He winked at Maddie. "Considering it's the home of the town baker."

His mother tilted her head. "What's that beeping noise?"

"The pies!" Maddie screamed and dashed toward the house. They raced after her.

"Dad!" Maddie yelled. "You were supposed to be listening for the timer."

Coach jumped off the sofa, but it was too late. Instead of golden, delectable crusts, the pies were black and charred.

She slumped against the sink. "They're ruined."

Her father gave a nervous chuckle. "You know what they say about the cobbler's children?"

She whirled on him. "What do they say about the cobbler's football-oblivious father, Dad?"

"That he is extremely sorry for letting his daughter down?" Coach rubbed his jaw. "Speaking of cobbler, though. You wouldn't happen to have any of that lying around, would you? Love me some apple right about now."

"You are unbelievable, you know that, Dad?"

Coach gave his daughter a tentative squeeze. "Unbelievably repentant yet still lovable?"

"Give me strength, but as a matter of fact..." She threw her father a stern look. "I could be persuaded to throw together a cobbler if the television is shut off and I get help with the peeling."

Coach nodded. "Done."

His mother smiled. "We'd love to help, too."

The apple cobbler—Maddie had a magical touch when it came to baking—was delicious.

It was late when he and his mom thanked the

Lovetts for their hospitality and prepared to head home. Already pulling out leftovers, Coach said his goodbyes from the kitchen.

Maddie walked them to the door. Bundled into her coat, his mother headed to the truck. His heart felt near to bursting. "This is the happiest I can remember seeing Mom in years."

"What about you, Tanner?"

He had the nearly irresistible urge to kiss her. But he didn't. Because win or lose, he wasn't planning on hanging out long-term in Truelove beyond football season.

"Did you enjoy spending Thanksgiving with us? With me?" she whispered.

He looked into her dark gaze and got a little lost there. "Today has been the happiest day for me, too."

But before he could say or do something he'd live to regret, he left her standing alone on the porch.

The kind of home—which he'd always longed for and never known—was exactly the sort of home he'd find with her.

Dearest God, I'm falling in love with Maddie, Coach's daughter.

Yanking open the truck door, he startled his mother. "Is everything all right, son?"

"Fine." Rocked within an inch of his life, he gritted his teeth and pulled away from the Lovett house. Away from what was best left alone.

Because needing someone like he was starting to need Maddie had never worked for him.

He'd learned early that vulnerability was a weakness best resisted. Steering out of the driveway, he darted a glance at his mother.

How could he dream of a future for himself when his mom depended on him so much? But that didn't mean a piece of his heart wouldn't forever remain in Truelove.

With a petite pastry chef who caused him to want a future that could never be his.

Chapter Eleven

Maddie spent the Friday after Thanksgiving filling a cake order for Maisie McAbee's tenth birthday.

Having transferred all the necessary ingredients from the bakery, she made the cake in her kitchen. Judging from the sculpted marzipan scissors and colored pencils that were requested, this year's birthday theme was arts and crafts.

Arriving at the house to pick up her order, Callie *ooh*ed and *aah*ed over the cake when it was completed. "This is a work of art. Maisie is going to adore it."

Maddie loved sharing the joy of milestone events in the lives of her Truelove neighbors.

"Feels like only yesterday, I was babysitting toddler Maisie with the adorable pink cowgirl boots so you and Jake could have a date night out."

"She loved those little boots." Callie sighed. "Now we have Micah, and another baby on the way."

Maddie carried the cake box out to Callie's car.

"Tonight, we're having five of Maisie's friends over for pizza, karaoke, crafts and cake."

"Sounds like the McAbees are in for a long night."

Callie chuckled. "I never believed the Double Name Club when they warned me how fast time passes with children, but they were right as usual."

Despite her busy, successful bakery, Maddie felt like she was still waiting for her life to begin.

"With the fourth-round football playoffs, it will be a long night for you and your dad, too. How is Coach?"

"Dad's as jittery about the game as a long-tailed cat on a porch full of rockers."

Her father wasn't going to the game, though. Not wishing to undermine Tanner's authority with the players and parents, he'd made the decision to forgo attending the rest of the season. But nervous tension was about to drive him—and her—over the edge.

She wrapped her hands in the sleeves of her purple heather cardigan. Late November was cold. Tonight would be bone-chilling.

But despite the freezing temps, she wouldn't miss being there to support Tanner at the away game for the world.

The dilemma about how to occupy her father sorted itself out. Her dad volunteered to hang out with ROMEO Ike Crenshaw at High Country Ranch so his son, Nate, and family could attend the game.

Several years ago, Ike had been diagnosed with early-onset dementia. When a service dog entered

Ike's life, Rascal's trainer and Nate's first love, Gemma, reentered Nate's life, too. Ike was doing great, but the Crenshaws didn't like to leave him home alone for too long.

In Truelove, neighbors helped neighbors. Maddie would go with her father to the ranch and hitch a ride to the game with Nate, Gemma and their young sons.

His driving privileges restored, her father was eager to get behind the wheel again. When she and her dad left the house, darkness had fallen across the valley.

The secondary road wound like stripes on a candy cane over the mountain.

He steered his truck toward the ranch. "I'm glad you're not driving to Jefferson."

"I'm not some flatlander tourist, Dad." She tucked her scarf inside her coat. "I can drive just fine over the mountains."

"Maybe so." He peered into the dark. Only a narrow guardrail separated the vehicle from the plunging gorge below. "But you'll always be my little girl."

Later, Maddie piled into the back seat between six-year-old Kody and his older brother, Connor. "I appreciate getting a lift to the game."

In the front seat, Gemma threw a smile at her husband. "It's not often my guys and I get the chance at a night out."

Kody told her about his 4H rabbits. Connor promised next time she came to the ranch, he'd let her feed the calf he was hand-raising. The forty-minute drive passed quickly.

As the visiting team, they joined other Truelove fans on the bleachers. Everyone came prepared with thermoses of hot chocolate. To ward off the biting wind whistling across the football field, Maddie wrapped a festive tartan throw around herself.

GeorgeAnne arrived with Tanner's mom. She gave GeorgeAnne and SandraLynn a couple of rechargeable hand warmers.

Shivering, SandraLynn thanked her and slipped the devices into her coat pockets to warm her hands. "I was always too nervous to watch Tanner play football in high school."

There was a strange desperate note to her voice.

Maddie's chest tightened. Everyone in Truelove knew the real reason SandraLynn never attended Tanner's games.

"I thought maybe now that he's coaching and not playing, it might be easier." SandraLynn moistened her lips. "But my stomach is in knots."

Maddie darted a look at GeorgeAnne.

The older woman shook her head. "Tanner can handle the pressure."

"Something he didn't inherit from me." SandraLynn laughed, but the sound lacked mirth.

GeorgeAnne patted her hand. "Our job is simple. We're here to cheer them on."

And cheer them on, they did. But Maddie worried about Tanner's mom. Yesterday, SandraLynn had seemed as if she was getting her life together. Tonight, she appeared emotionally wobbly.

Maybe SandraLynn wasn't doing as well as she pretended. Over the last few months, she'd made so many positive changes in her life. Maddie hated to see that go to waste.

Just before the first quarter ended, SandraLynn excused herself to find the restroom.

"Maybe I should—"

GeorgeAnne laid her gnarled hand on Maddie's coat sleeve. "We're not her wardens."

The Double Name Club leader forced a smile. "How much trouble can she get into at a high school football game?"

But Maddie knew better. Trouble didn't have to find SandraLynn Price. Too often, she went looking for it.

"If she falls off the wagon, Tanner will be devastated." Maddie knotted her fingers.

GeorgeAnne's breath fogged in the brisk night air. "SandraLynn was always too pretty for her own good. Her parents were older when she was born. They gave her everything, except the life skills she'd need when life stopped going her way."

"Like when Tanner's father walked out?"

GeorgeAnne nodded. "SandraLynn always struggled with pride. He left her for a younger woman."

"Should I mention my concerns to Tanner?"

GeorgeAnne pursed her lips. "Tanner can be extremely defensive about his mom. I'd think long and hard before opening that can of worms."

"You think we should trust SandraLynn to keep her word to Tanner?"

GeorgeAnne's brow furrowed. "I think we should trust Tanner to do what he thinks is best for his mother."

Just then, SandraLynn returned to the bleachers. Hardly an expert on inebriation, Maddie couldn't tell if his mom's flushed cheeks and red nose were the result of the cold air or from something else entirely.

She had a bad feeling. And she felt that if sharing her doubts prevented his mom from regressing, Tanner would thank her.

During halftime, she left GeorgeAnne and SandraLynn to chat and ran into newlyweds Chloe and Noah. Chloe invited her to join a group of them tomorrow at the Christmas parade.

"Feel free to invite Tanner." Chloe winked. "'Cause I know you want to."

"Maybe I will." She fought to keep a grin off her face. "Maybe I won't."

"Been there, done that, girl. But admit it. You've got it bad for Truelove's stand-in football coach."

She opened her mouth to deny it, but a blush betrayed her. "I guess I do." It felt good to admit it out loud.

"The team's not all I'm rooting for, dear friend. I'm pulling for you and Tanner to find your happily-ever-after, too."

Maddie threw her a side-eye. "Still working on earning your matchmaker credentials, I see."

Chloe laughed. "I'm still hoping to help Ingrid find her perfect match."

"Just so long as the veterinarian's perfect match isn't the stand-in football coach."

Chloe gave a long-suffering sigh. "Thus far, my beautiful friend seems to be nobody's perfect match." The veterinarian was notoriously prickly.

An interesting look flitted across Chloe's features. "Why haven't the matchmakers made an effort to get you hitched?"

It *was* odd she hadn't fallen into their clutches.

Chloe nudged her. "They're probably afraid if they make you mad, you'll cut them off from those to-die-for lemon bars."

"GeorgeAnne does love those sweet treats."

Her compatriots in matrimonial mischief, ErmaJean and IdaLee, were equally passionate about Maddie's cherry tarts and the ever-delectable Neiman Marcus cookies.

Chloe snorted. "Who would have guessed Madeline's would prove to be the kryptonite to their matchmaking superpowers?"

The last two quarters of the game were a close match, but Truelove emerged victorious. Afterward, Tanner sent the guys to the visitor bleachers to thank everyone for coming out in the cold to lend their support.

Just one of the many things he did to create a place in the hearts of Truelove residents.

He'd certainly created a special place in hers.

She'd started daring to dream when—not if,

loyal Bobcat fan that she was—the team won the state championship, the school board might cough up funds to hire an assistant coach to help her father next year.

Might Tanner reconsider his career choices and decide to stay in Truelove?

She made her way to the sidelines. "Congratulations, Coach Price."

Staring at his clipboard, Tanner didn't say anything.

Maddie smiled. "Next stop, regionals."

His head snapped up. "I'm well aware, Maddie. I don't need any added pressure from you."

Despite the win, he was obviously not in the greatest of moods. Got it.

She recalled his odd reaction on the porch last night. He'd appeared to be having a great time with her. Until he wasn't.

He scowled. "If that's all, I need to get to the team bus." Turning on his heel, he strode across the field toward the parking lot.

A trifle gobsmacked, she stared at his back a second before charging after him. "Actually, that wasn't all." She had to run to keep up with his long strides. "Chloe and Noah are getting together a group to watch the Christmas parade tomorrow and invited you to join us."

He wheeled around so suddenly, she teetered in her boots. "Despite what everyone seems to think, the only reason I returned to Truelove was to take care of my mother. The only reason I'm still here—" his chest heaved "—is because I'm repaying a debt of honor to the Truelove High football program."

She opened her hands in a conciliatory gesture. "I just thought you might like to blow off steam with friends."

"Other than teammates, I had no friends in Truelove. There's my fair-weather girlfriends, though." His mouth twisted. "Are you expecting Haley or Jessica or Brianna to join the parade watchers?"

Her cheeks stung from more than the cold. With his golden arm, Tanner had been a big man on campus his entire high school career. With football glory came cheerleaders.

All her insecurities came flooding back.

He clutched the clipboard to his jacket. "If you'll excuse me, I'd like to speak to my mother before Walter takes her home."

She ignored the dozen or so flashing red warning lights in her head. "About your mother."

"What about my mother?"

"Are you sure Miss SandraLynn is as okay as you think?"

His eyes narrowed. "What do you mean?"

"Never mind." She would have walked away, but he caught her arm.

Maddie's gaze flicked to the not-quite-empty bleachers. Their raised voices and her undignified sprint had gained them unwanted attention.

"You've got something you want to say, so say it, Maddie."

She swallowed. "I'm concerned SandraLynn isn't coping as well as any of us would like to believe. Maybe she's not as sober as you hope."

His eyes flashed. "Have you seen her take a drink?"

"No," she whispered.

"My mother's sobriety is none of your business," he hissed.

He jabbed his index finger in the frosty air between them. "You were the last person I would've ever believed would throw stones at a woman who's working desperately hard to rebuild her life."

Stalking toward the bus, he left Maddie blinking away tears and shaking with utter misery.

GeorgeAnne had been right. She should have never said anything about his mom. He wanted so badly to believe his mother was okay.

But despite any concrete evidence, her instincts were screaming that something was very much amiss with SandraLynn's recovery.

With a sinking sense of dread, she couldn't shake the feeling that disaster loomed on the horizon. Threatening to demolish any foolish hopes and dreams she might harbor.

Tanner was ashamed of giving Maddie the brush-off at the game.

But on her porch the other night, his feelings for her had scared him. He'd needed to put some emotional distance between them. It had been a low blow throwing the cheerleaders in her face. Those girls had been catty and so beneath someone of Maddie's caliber.

The only reason they'd given him the time of day had been to bask in his gridiron glory. After the injury at the university, Brianna had dumped him so fast it had made his head spin.

Maddie was the only one who ever cared about him—the real him. The only one who'd ever seen him as someone worth more than the points he could put on a scoreboard.

Tanner was ashamed of raising his voice to Maddie, but her unfounded accusations against his mom triggered a host of fears about the possibility of his mother relapsing. Again.

However, throughout the remainder of Thanksgiving weekend, he found himself looking for any telltale signs his mom wasn't as sober as he'd hoped.

Yet whatever Maddie had suspected at the football game, his mother rose Saturday morning energetic and eager to "do Christmas right this year."

He took her to the Morgan Christmas tree farm. Along with what felt like half of Truelove, he let her select the tree of her Christmas dreams.

They spent a fun afternoon decorating it. They laughed a lot. She smiled a lot.

Standing under the glowing lights of the Fraser fir, his mom was like a little girl again. Caught up in the magic of Christmas. He shut his mind against the doubts Maddie had raised.

He was far less enthused when his mother suggested venturing downtown for hot apple cider, courtesy of the Mason Jar, to see the kids visit Santa on the Square.

"Is GeorgeAnne still dressing up in that green elf costume?"

His mother clapped her hands together. "That's worth the price of admission alone."

One of the big civic events of the year, the mayor played Santa. Miss IdaLee usually was Mrs. Claus.

If it made his mother happy, though, why not go? The parade was long over. Maddie and her friends were probably long gone.

His mother's blue eyes twinkled. "You can give Santa your Christmas wish list, Tan-Tan."

Tanner kissed her forehead. "My Christmas wishes have already come true, Mom."

In the historic gazebo, Santa and his missus perched on a red velvet throne. Loudspeakers piped strains of "Winter Wonderland."

His mother sighed. "If only it would snow."

"If you're hoping for a white Christmas, better put in your wish today, Mom."

All his guys—weird how he'd started thinking of the team that way—and their families kept stopping in the square to shake his hand.

His mother squeezed his arm. "I'm so proud of you, son."

"I'm proud of you, too, Mom."

For a split second, something flickered in her gaze. So brief as to be almost nonexistent. But his breath caught.

Letting go of him, his mother moved to get a cup of steaming apple cider from one of the staff in front of the Mason Jar.

He caught a gander at GeorgeAnne on the steps of the gazebo. Exercising her firmly held belief she must run every occasion in Truelove, she organized the line of children waiting to speak to dear old Saint Nick.

Tanner's gaze landed on Maddie and friends hanging out near the center of the green.

Her friends appeared to mainly consist of men and the cool blond veterinarian. The lady vet was inarguably attractive but about as warm as a frozen fish stick. He recognized Chloe's two older brothers, Jeffrey and Travis. The lanky guy—Zach?—owned the auto repair shop in town.

He apparently said something so witty that Maddie laughed helplessly against him. Tanner gritted his teeth. The mechanic was obviously far better with words than him.

Tanner's blood did a slow boil.

A few grades ahead of Tanner, Zach was way too old to be interested in Maddie. Tanner tightened his jaw.

Back in the day, the dude had been crazy into car racing. Friendly as a cocker spaniel. Everybody's best bud, something Zach and Maddie had in common.

Tanner's stomach roiled.

He had an inherent distrust of people who felt

the need to smile all the time. Get real. Nobody was happy all the time.

What could they possibly find to smile about all the time?

His mom thrust a cup of cider at him. "Is everything okay?"

"Never better," he growled.

Taking a large gulp, he immediately had regrets. The hot cider burned all the way down. Not unlike his simmering mood.

He had no desire to watch the mechanic flirt with the petite pastry chef. *His* pastry chef.

Tanner sputtered. Not his pastry chef. Not his anything.

His mother pounded on his back. "Sure you're okay?"

Heads turned. Nosy busybody Truelove.

Tanner chucked the cup in a nearby receptacle. "I think I'd prefer to spend a quiet evening at home with you."

That week, he poured himself into his work. Classes in the morning. Football practice in the afternoons.

In an effort to stop thinking about Maddie—a losing battle—he drilled the team and drove himself hard.

Preston and the rest of the study hall kids were making real progress with the robot. Tanner managed to leverage the football team's success into creating interest—and funds—for his robotic team so they could travel to Houston for the national competition in April.

He'd be long gone by then, but he was proud of their creativity and skills. And he told them so.

People ought to be more concerned about building a kid's confidence. The teen years were tough. A guy like Preston—like Tanner back in the day—needed all the boosting they could get.

He liked working with students. Who would have seen that coming?

Tanner liked the teenagers' enthusiasm. The quirky way they looked at the world. Heartbreakingly honest and yet sometimes laugh-out-loud comical. Often at the same time.

He'd decided from bitter personal experience to be the kind of teacher he always wished he'd had. He'd had Coach in his corner. And Maddie.

Tanner's gut ached a little.

After what happened Friday night, she probably hated him. Hers was the only true friendship he'd ever had—and he'd managed to destroy that, too.

Like he ruined every relationship with anyone he got close to. He was a walking catastrophe. There should be public service warnings surrounding him.

He gave up early-morning runs to Madeline's. Yet despite avoiding her, every night he dreamed about her. Each night, the dreams got worse.

First he dreamed he ran into Maddie and the mechanic on a date at the Burger Barn. Then, in another dream, they got married. Worst dream of all, Zach put his hand on her belly and Tanner realized she was carrying his child.

His heart hammering out of his chest, he awoke drenched in sweat. A vague sense of impending doom threatened to swallow him whole.

The last dream was probably triggered by hearing that Kara MacKenzie finally had her baby girl. It had been all over the Jar when he went for his usual can't-do-cafeteria lunch.

Truelove's tiniest new citizen, born on December 1 and befitting her mother's love of all things French and Christmas, was named Noèle Marie MacKenzie.

It was Kara's father-in-law, ROMEO Rick, who mentioned her brothers would be visiting the new mom and baby. He also suggested the brothers—all former all-star ACC offensive linemen turned successful corporate execs of their mother's barbecue chain—might be persuaded to give the team an inspirational pep talk before the regional final on Friday night.

A genius idea.

Mama G looked on with maternal pride as her sons, Cedrick and Terence Ferguson, spoke to the football team Thursday night at the Jar.

They were down to earth yet *GQ* polished. Cedrick had spent a few years in the NFL. Like Preston and the majority of mountain kids, most of the Truelove High football players had never been out of the state, much less on an airplane. Kara's intelligent, hardworking, totally cool brothers expanded the boys' vision of what could be.

In a nutshell, that was what he found so exciting and fulfilling about working with students.

He could see younger versions of Randall, DaShonte, Hurley and Javier in those men. And more importantly, they could see themselves in the Fergusons, too.

Not just men who could pass or catch a football. But men of integrity, family and faith.

The kind of man he aspired to be. The sort of man Maddie made him want to be. But instead, he'd failed her. And himself.

She did not attend team-building night, which both relieved and upset him. Instead, she sent shortbread cookies in the shape of footballs, the stitched laces decorated with white icing, via IdaLee.

He was able to get his sugar fix. His Maddie fix—not so much.

Friday afternoon, he was in a dark mood when he boarded the bus to head to the West Regional game against the number two–ranked school in their class division, the Black Knights. It was nearly a four-hour drive to Graham County.

Pleading a headache, his mom opted not to make the trip with GeorgeAnne. Their neighbor offered to stay home with her, but his mother insisted GeorgeAnne take her place in cheering her son to victory.

GeorgeAnne wasn't happy about it. Neither was he. But he wasn't the only one who'd had a trying week. Several nights after work, his mom had come home frazzled and inexplicably near the end of her rope.

Renewed doubts about her sobriety played at the frayed edges of his mind.

On the interminable journey, he had way too much time to second-guess game strategy and fret over the lack of pastry in his life.

Local sports commentators were already calling Truelove the year's Cinderella team. He was wary of what unearned accolades could do to a kid's head. Gruffly, he barked orders left and right as the players got off the bus.

"Quit goofing around, DaShonte." He jerked his thumb at Javier. "That equipment isn't going to unload itself, Diaz."

"Yes, Coach."

"Sure thing, Coach."

"On it, Coach."

He made sure the guys understood nothing in life was a cake walk. Regionals were serious business.

When the going gets tough, the truly tough get the job done. And they had a job to do—to win.

It was a close one. But they pulled off another win. He'd been so laser-focused, it was only after the game he realized how many fans had made the trek with them from town.

Truelove loved its football and their players. Their hometown coaches, too.

Swept along in the euphoria of the moment, he was taken aback by the jubilation. And judging from the hearty claps on his shoulders, the town's respect.

Against his will, his gaze scanned the bleachers. Looking for—hoping against hope—a glimpse of Maddie. Her loyalty to the team predated any tie to him. Had she come?

There. Top left. Sitting between the Stone family, who owned the dude ranch, and ErmaJean Hicks, Bill's lady love.

In her red coat and scarf, she looked a sight for sore eyes. However, the white knit cap was entirely inadequate to contain those dark, riotous curls of hers.

To dispel the sudden remembered feel of those silken strands between his fingers, he clenched his fists.

She turned her head. The curls danced over her shoulder. His breath quickened. Her gaze—somehow as if he'd willed it—found his and locked.

He forced himself to smile. An olive branch.

Which she neither accepted, acknowledged nor returned.

Instead, she rose. Clanked down the bleachers. Ground level, she turned her back on him.

Stars exploded in front of his eyes. This couldn't be happening. Blindsided and aghast, his stomach dropped to the turf beneath his feet.

Sweet little Maddie *Never Hold a Grudge* Lovett had dissed him. Not unlike how he'd very publicly turned his back on her last Friday night. It was no more than he deserved.

Was this the end for him and Maddie?

But he summoned the dogged pigheadedness that propelled him in spite of a learning disability and past thwarted dreams of football glory to a successful career.

He wouldn't let this be the end of their lifelong friendship.

On the long ride back to Truelove, he had plenty of time to strategize his next play.

Maddie Lovett never missed a community event. The annual tree-lighting was this Sunday night on the square. He would make it his business to be there.

She deserved a real apology. Heartfelt, sincere and public. One for the record books, an apology she'd not soon forget.

Nor Truelove, either.

He could fix this. He absolutely could.

And he would.

Chapter Twelve

Maddie spent the wee hours of Saturday morning putting the finishing touches on the Green twins' eleventh-birthday cake.

Befitting those particularly boisterous preteens, the theme was a veritable explosion of color. Festooned with as much razzmatazz sparkle, cheetah prints, neon marzipan and frenetic energy as she could translate onto a cake.

She didn't have to spend the darkest hours before dawn sculpting the cake. But after the upsetting non-exchange with Tanner, she was a wreck.

Maddie found a place for the cake in her commercial-size garage fridge.

Returning to the kitchen, she turned out a batch of sourdough onto the floured counter and went to work kneading it.

It wasn't like her to be rude. Her instinct was always to turn the other cheek, restore and reconcile.

She hated conflict—bent over backward, went out of her way to avoid even a semblance of discord. But not this time. She punched the ball of dough with her fist.

Not This Time, Tanner Price.

At the memory of how she'd chased after him across the football field like a silly, lovesick fool, her cheeks heated. But no more. She thwacked the dough with the rolling pin.

No More, Tanner Price.

She resolved to avoid him for the duration of his Truelove tenure.

No biggie. She had enjoyed a perfectly lovely life before he swanned back into town.

She would have a perfectly lovely life again, despite Tanner Price, long after he crept his way out of town once more.

From now on it would be full-price pastries for him. Or maybe she'd cut him off altogether.

Nah. Kara had taught her to be a better businesswoman than that. A dollar was a dollar.

She gathered the shreds of her professionalism around her like a mantle.

Two more games—*God willing*—tops. They would each spend the height of the holiday season with their families. Then this little blast from the past would reach its inevitable conclusion.

Which was exactly how it had always been, should and forever more would be. Amen.

"Maddie, honey?" Bleary-eyed and in his pjs, her father staggered into the kitchen. "Is everything all right?"

Rolling pin poised over the uncooperative dough, she blinked at him. "Whatever gave you the idea something was wrong?"

He shuffled his slippered feet. "Maybe the sounds of mortal combat taking place out here?"

She slumped against the island. "I didn't mean to wake you." She heaved the overstretched, overworked dough into the trash can.

Like Tanner Price, another massive waste of her time and energy.

"Maddie?"

She waved her hand. "Go back to bed. I promise to bake more quietly."

"You know if there's anything troubling you, Maddie girl, you can talk to me. Nothing on this earth is more important to me than you."

She came out from around the counter and threw her arms around him. "I know, Dad. I'm fine."

Or she would be once she moved past her stupid, unrequited feelings for Tanner.

"Get some sleep, honey."

"I need to straighten up the kitchen and I'll be right behind you, Dad."

Having worked off some of her fury on the innocent dough, she fell into bed, exhausted and spent, soon after. High emotional drama always had that effect on her.

The next morning, she awoke in a much better frame of mind. It wasn't in her nature to stay down in the dumps for long. Not when she had so much good work to do and wonderful things in her life to look forward to.

On today's baking list, she had to put the finishing touches on a cake for a big Christmas shindig at the Birchfield event venue later tonight.

At noon, Preston stopped by to pick up the cake for the Green twins. How had she ever run her business without him? Managing the three-tiered cake was a trickier proposition. Preston would need help. She went with him to deliver the confectionary creation to Kelsey.

Sunday, her day of rest from baking, meant going to church with her dad and then lunch. Later, she popped into the MacKenzies' to meet Kara's beautiful baby girl.

Around three o'clock, her dad left to watch the Sunday-afternoon NFL game with buddies. She'd promised to meet Chloe and friends at the Christmas tree lighting.

As twilight fell across the valley, she was pleased to find an empty parking space on the Lyric Arts Center side of the green.

Crossing on foot to the square, she called greetings to groups of townsfolk and searched the crowd for Chloe and company.

Thanks to the continuing efforts of the matchmakers, singles like Maddie were becoming an endangered species.

Before her marriage, Chloe had formed the group partly as a defense mechanism, and also for her fledging matchmaking endeavors on behalf of Ingrid. They were a fun group. Maddie enjoyed hanging out with them.

It did her self-esteem no harm when Chloe's

brothers, Jeffrey and Travis, firefighter Tate Bradley and Zach's face lit up at the sight of her.

Take that, Tanner Price. Some people thought her attractive. She was pleased she'd made the effort with her appearance.

Not that she'd done it for Tanner. Somebody as anti-social as Tanner wouldn't bother attending something as small-town festive as the tree lighting. There was no danger she'd run into him. And she was glad of it.

Joining her friends, she almost convinced herself she meant it.

Tanner spent Saturday composing and rehearsing his apology to Maddie. The final result hit just the right balance between sincere and remorseful.

On paper, everything looked promising. Though the written word wasn't his strong suit, overall he felt good about how she would respond.

Come Monday morning, he was anticipating a resumption of coffee, croissants and camaraderie with her at Madeline's.

Heading downtown, he was in a great mood. The only fly in the ointment was when his mother had declined to accompany him to the tree lighting.

Smiling, she wagged her finger at him. "Christmas is not the time to be too nosy. I have gifts to wrap."

He didn't press his mom for further details because it would be easier to talk to Maddie if he was alone.

Just like the weekend before, the square was packed with Truelove citizens. A huge Fraser fir—from Luke Morgan's tree farm—had been placed in front of the gazebo.

Excitement buzzed like electricity across the square. Awaiting the ceremonial flip of the switch by Mayor Watson, children darted around family and friends. Hoping to spot Maddie, he took a position next to one of the softly lit cast-iron lampposts lining the walkways of the green.

Tanner saw Lili first, sitting on Noah's shoulders so she could see better above the heads of the crowd. Chloe and her brothers stood beside them. But it was Maddie's red coat which captured his attention. She stood out like a cheery cardinal against the green boughs of the magnolia tree behind her.

He was less thrilled to find her talking, her cheeks rosy from the cold, with Zach Stone.

Did the guy have no one else to hang out with other than Maddie?

Sweet Maddie was too polite to rebuff his unwelcome attentions. Unless, of course, she actually liked him back.

For a second, the idea she might be into the dude was a gut-check. But common sense prevailed. No way she had a thing for Zach. The very notion was ridiculous. She could do so much better than him.

Just like she could do so much better than Tanner.

Scrubbing his hand over his face, he decided to wait until the tree lighting was over. He'd catch

Maddie on her way to her car. After she'd ditched the mechanic.

But Maddie's very animated conversation with the mechanic grated on his last nerve. Feeling a slow burn, he crossed his arms over his chest.

Zach was really hee-hawing it up over there. She appeared to be soaking it in like an April rain on parched desert soil.

He gritted his teeth. Shuffled his feet. Practiced exhaling for three breaths. Inhaling for three.

Then his eyes almost bugged out of his head.

Stone brushed Maddie's curls off her shoulder. How dare he?

Of their own volition, his feet took a step forward. And another. Pushing through the crowd. Until he came face-to-face with Maddie.

"Hi, Tanner." She gave him a fleeting uncertain smile. "I didn't think I'd see—"

"We need to talk."

A line appeared in the space between her perfect eyebrows and cute little nose. "After the tree—"

"Now," he grunted.

Her gaze darted to Chloe and back to him. "We were waiting for—"

"I'm not waiting." He took her hand and glared at Stone.

Zach caught hold of her other arm. "Maybe the lady doesn't want to talk to you right now."

For a moment, she stood between them. "I—I..."

Was the mechanic right? His chest pinched. Maybe she didn't want him in her life anymore?

Unlike Stone's wiry lankiness, Tanner was solid muscle. He could absolutely take him if push came to shove, but... what was he doing? This wasn't the man he wanted to be.

His grip on her hand loosened. "I'm sorry. I shouldn't have—"

But her fingers tightened around his. "It's okay."

Renewed hope surged through his veins. He threw a pointed look at Zach, who hadn't dropped his hand from her arm.

Chloe's older brother, Travis, a highway patrolman wounded last year in the line of duty, put his hand on Zach's shoulder. "Let her go with him, man."

Zach let go of her arm, and Tanner guided her through the crowd, searching for a quiet space so he could apologize.

Just as the mayor stepped to the mic, an unexpected gap opened before Tanner. Surging forward, he drew her to the edge of the crowd to one of the mulched borders lining the base of the gazebo.

Tanner kept his fingers twined in hers. But as the opportunity arose to apologize, his mind blanked.

"He's too old for you, Maddie," he blurted.

She blinked at him. "What?"

The mayor droned on.

"With your father not at his best, I feel it's my duty to look out for you."

"Your *duty*?" Her eyebrows rose nearly to her hairline. "You are not my father, Tanner."

"Of course not, I'm your friend." He nodded. "Which is why—"

"My friend?"

Why did she keep repeating what he said? Was he not being clear?

"Is that what we are, Tanner? Friends?"

His brow furrowed. Communication was key. Hence, the painstakingly crafted apology.

"I apologize for how I acted at regionals."

She folded her arms across her coat. "After I shared my concerns with you regarding your mother." She sniffed. "As your friend."

When she put it like that... Yet there could be no comparison between him looking out for her and her accusations against his mom.

"No." He scowled. "Yes. Maybe."

This was not going the way he envisioned. He wasn't sure exactly how the conversation had derailed, nor how to get their friendship back on track. Maybe homing in on Zach hadn't been the wisest play.

He fumbled in his jeans pocket for the statement he'd prepared.

"What are you doing?"

Tanner lifted his head. "I was afraid of forgetting what I wanted to say so I wrote it down." He brandished the three-by-five notecard. "One of the academic tricks you taught me, remember? Throughout my life, it's come in surprisingly handy."

He read aloud his heartfelt sentiment regarding the value he placed on their friendship.

Tanner laid out a calm, unemotional argument for why for the sake of their friendship, anything more between them wasn't sensible. He reiterated the temporary nature of his return, which was the complete opposite of her, Truelove's forever hometown girl.

He cited his far-flung career. How he wasn't serious relationship-material. How he was doing her a favor.

Then he glanced up.

He was slightly taken aback at the heightened color in her cheeks. Why was she mad with him when he was trying to fix their—

"That's what you wanted to—" Her dark eyes glinted with fury. "—no, what you *demanded* to talk to me about?"

"Well, yeah."

He frowned. Had she heard the part about how much he valued her in his life?

"Unbelievable." She rolled her eyes. "This is your idea of an apology? You dragged me away from my friends because—"

"Because the mechanic was getting inappropriate."

Her mouth dropped. "Zach has never been anything other than a perfect gentleman." Her lips twisted. "And if he was, it's certainly no business of yours, Tanner Price." She jerked free. "I've had it up to here with your moods. You can get right off that high horse you're riding. It won't slice bread with me."

Tanner scuffed the toe of his boot into the grass. "I just—"

She rounded on him. "You just can't see me as anything other than Coach's little girl, can you?" She jabbed her finger in his chest.

Flinching he rubbed the spot. "I don't—"

"Who I choose to befriend is none of your business. Despite wanting to be my big brother—"

"I don't want to be your brother," he growled.

"Then what is it you want from me, Tanner?"

Staring at her, he was vaguely aware of the mayor beginning the countdown and the crowd chiming in. *One...*

The accumulated, frustrated longings of dozens of sleepless nights and empty days rose inside him.

She threw out her hands. "This is exactly what I expected you to not say."

Two...

She turned to walk away, but he caught her hand.

"This is what I want, Maddie." Cradling her head, he placed his hands on either side of her face. "This."

When he touched his mouth against hers, he felt her sudden intake of breath. Had he scared her?

He drew back a fraction. Did she not want him to—

Leaning into him, her arms went around his neck. She kissed him back. The sweetness of it slammed into him. The rightness. The sense of finding and coming home.

Then he wasn't capable of further rational thought.

He'd kissed other women before. But this was Maddie. It was so much more than he'd ever believed possible.

Three...

As the lights on the Christmas tree sprang to life, so, too, did the footlights at the base of the gazebo.

Snared in the glare of the spotlight, they broke apart. He shielded his eyes with his hand.

To better see the Christmas tree, most people had their backs to them. But GeorgeAnne and her Double Name ladies chose that moment to glance their way. Several of his football team players, too. Kyle had the nerve to snicker.

Tanner put himself between her, the spotlight and the rubberneckers. "Shut it, Wadsworth." He shot the freshman kicker a look that boded ill for future drills.

"Oh..." She did her best to pat her hair into a semblance of order. Her knit cap was askew. Her tangled curls was his fault entirely. "I—I..."

Finding herself a public spectacle, she took a step, poised to flee. The world, he noticed, was a colder place without her in his arms.

She stumbled over the mulch. Taking her elbow, he helped her step off the mounded border and onto the path.

"Wait, Maddie..." He plunged down the walkway after her. "Please, stop."

She stopped so abruptly he plowed into her.

She would have fallen flat on her face if he hadn't snagged her about the waist and held her upright against his chest.

"Talk to me, Maddie. Tell me what you're feeling. Would you look at me? Maddie?"

But she shook her head. The silk of her hair brushed his cheekbone. His heart went into overdrive.

"You didn't have to come after me." In her voice was a whisper of tears, only just held at bay. "I understand. I truly do. You're under so much pressure right now."

She fluttered her hand. "We'll chalk it up to the heat of the moment. Temporary insanity. To Christmas."

"But I'm not sorry," he whispered into her hair. The scent of vanilla teased at his nostrils. "Just the opposite."

She turned in his arms. "But you friend-zoned me."

He thought he might drown in the big, dark well of her eyes. "You and I, Maddie..." He gulped. "We are definitely not in the friend zone."

"What does that mean?"

His heart thundered. "It means I want to kiss you again."

"What about your job?"

He shrugged. "Which one?"

"The one that'll take you far, far away from Truelove."

"I honestly don't know what the future holds for

me. For us. And you are still way too good for the likes of me."

"Stop saying that." She put her hand on his cheek. "It isn't true."

But it was.

"I like you, Maddie Lovett. Way too much." Far more than made him comfortable. Far more than he was ready to acknowledge.

She tilted her head. "I like you, too, Tanner Price." Blushing, she dropped her gaze. "As I believe my previous actions attempted to demonstrate."

He lifted her chin with the tip of his finger. "I can't make you any promises, Mads."

"I'm not asking for any."

"But I'm willing to explore the possibilities if you're willing to go there with me."

Suddenly, only a breath stood between them again.

"We'll take it one game at a time." As featherlight as a butterfly's wings, she brushed her lips against his cheek. "One kiss at a time."

"Like your eclairs, I think I'm going to need more than one."

She smiled. "Aren't you afraid of attracting a crowd?"

"For all I care, Truelove can sell tickets." Grinning, he kissed her again.

Chapter Thirteen

The week that followed the tree lighting was the best of Maddie's life.

With lots of holiday parties, business was brisk, but it was the time she and Tanner spent together that made the week so wonderful.

Arriving early each morning, he was always her first customer. "Put me to work," he'd say.

So she did. When he donned a Madeline's apron over his dress shirt, she laughed until she cried. But he proved a deft hand at serving customers and ringing up orders.

It was fun working with him behind the counter.

"You may find yourself with a new career."

He smiled. "Maybe I need a new career."

Was he thinking about changing jobs? Was he considering relocating to Truelove on a permanent basis?

Her heart leaped in her chest. But she was careful to keep her voice evenly modulated.

Now they were official, Tanner asked her to go to dinner with him Wednesday night at an upscale Italian restaurant in downtown Asheville.

Despite having known each other since they were teenagers, she was a nervous wreck getting ready for him to pick her up after football practice.

She changed clothes twice. She fiddled with her hair for over forty minutes until finally admitting defeat. Her curls had a mind of their own.

Her father leaned against the doorframe of her bedroom. "You look beautiful, Maddie girl."

Sitting on the bench in front of her vanity, she grimaced at her reflection in the mirror. "I look like I stuck my finger into a socket."

"Not true. I have the feeling Tanner would remain smitten even if you put a burlap bag over your head."

"Burlap might actually be an improvement."

He rolled his eyes. "I've never seen you so worked up over a date, baby doll."

"This is Tanner." She turned on the bench. "You don't mind about Tanner and me going out, do you?"

"Tanner called me last night before he asked you to dinner."

She placed her hands on her knees. "And?"

"You like him a lot, don't you?"

She sighed. "More than a lot, Dad."

"He's a good guy, but his background is…challenging."

"You mean SandraLynn's situation."

"Most of his life, his mother's impossible emotional demands put him between a rock and a hard place through no fault of his own." Her dad pursed his lips. "I don't want to see you get hurt."

She didn't want to get hurt, either. "I'm going into this with my eyes wide open."

"That's wise." He folded his arms over his chest. "Long as he treats you right, Tanner and I will have no issue."

She didn't feel wise. Despite the many obstacles standing between them, not the least of which was his mother's illness and his job, she couldn't live with herself if she didn't give their growing relationship a fair chance.

Yet she also felt vulnerable and terrified. Everything between them felt so lovely and new and very, very fragile. She never wanted this time with him to end.

But each night, a gnawing uncertainty awoke her. She feared happiness, like shifting sand, would slip through her fingers.

By the time Tanner left to pick her up, he'd changed his shirt twice. His tie, three times.

Genuinely pleased for him, his mom pushed him out the door. "You don't want to be late."

He picked up Maddie at her house. Wearing a lacy dark-plum-colored dress, she was a complete knockout. Asheville was about an hour's drive from Truelove.

"Such a classy place." She gazed around the candlelit taverna. "I would've been happy at the Burger

Barn." She smiled at him across the table. "As long as it was with you."

His heart turned over in his chest. "Our first real date called for something more momentous."

"First?" Her dark eyes sparkled. "There's you assuming there's going to be more than one."

"I wanted to impress you."

"You've always impressed me, Tanner." She tilted her head. "In ways that have absolutely nothing to do with football."

"Enough to earn me a second date?"

Her lips curved. "I believe something could be arranged."

It was one of the most wonderful evenings of his life.

That night, he confined himself to one gentle, good-night kiss on her doorstep. He was determined to show her the respect she deserved. He wanted to be the kind of guy she deserved.

During the week of the regional playoff, once Ann arrived to man the bakery, he and Maddie often braved the cold. Taking their coffees, they did a quick circuit of the usually deserted square until he had to report to school. He even shared his cinnamon roll with her.

They talked. They laughed. He never wanted their time together to end. Which prompted a reevaluation of his life.

After Coach returned to his job, was there a way Tanner could stay in Truelove? Was there another job for which he might be qualified and earn a decent living?

There wasn't only his future with Maddie to consider. With his mom sober, he longed to recapture the years alcohol had stolen from them.

Hope, as unfamiliar as it was new, filled him.

The regional game was a nail-biter, but running back DaShonte pulled out a last-minute touchdown to win the game.

During the final week before the state championship, a cold, torrential downpour cancelled Monday-afternoon practice on the field. Instead, he reviewed game tape and strategy with the team.

Feeling good about their readiness for the upcoming championship game, he decided to surprise his mom at the pharmacy.

She ought to be getting off soon. The calendar in the pantry had indicated she was working days this week. Maybe they could catch the early bird special at the restaurant across the street.

But her car wasn't in the parking lot. Inside the store, she was nowhere to be found. He flagged down a clerk, his mom's long-time coworker.

The older woman wouldn't meet his gaze. "We miss SandraLynn a lot, Tanner."

"What are you talking about?"

The woman fiddled with her name badge. "SandraLynn doesn't work here anymore."

He stared at her. "Since when?"

She bit her lip. "The week after Thanksgiving."

"That was three weeks ago," he gasped. "What happened?"

"SandraLynn was a no-show for so many shifts. I tried to cover for her. That last day she made it to work, but she wasn't herself."

"You mean she was drunk." Which also meant his mother had driven to work in that state.

"The manager had given her so many warnings, but that was the last straw." She looked at him. "I'm sorry."

So was he.

If his mother wasn't going to work, where had she been going every day for the last three weeks while he was at school?

He went home. Her sedan was parked in its usual place. He put his hand on the engine hood. It was warm. If practice hadn't been cut short, he would have never known anything was amiss.

Anger churned his gut. He stormed into the house and caught her in the kitchen in the act of downing a shot of liquor.

She bolted to her feet. "Tanner?" Her bloodshot eyes darted to the bottle. "You're home early. I—"

"You swore you were done drinking. You've not only lost your job, but you're driving drunk now, too? Seriously?"

Unsteady on her feet, she drew herself up. "I don't have to answer to you."

"You don't answer to anyone except the irresistible call of the next drink." His mouth twisted.

"What happened to only drinking on the weekend, Ma? Forget what day of the week it is? Or are the days all running together now?"

Whatever semblance of control she ever possessed under the influence, she lost. Raining abuse on him, she called him every name in the book and then some.

Stunned, he gaped at her. He'd never seen her this way.

When she finally stopped—to take another drink—he walked out of the house. She was too far gone to notice.

He drove around aimlessly for a while. As dusk drew the blanket of night over the valley, he found himself pulling into the church. Reverend Bryant crossed the footbridge to the parking lot.

Spotting him, the pastor tapped on the truck window. "Is everything all right?"

Nothing was all right.

"Can I help you, son?"

He recalled the snippet of information Maddie told him about Reverend Bryant. Pain built inside his chest.

He opened the truck door and got out. "You're on your way home, sir."

"Supper will keep." Reverend Bryant put his hand on his shoulder. "Let's talk."

In the pastor's study, for the first time in his life, Tanner said the words out loud. "My mother is an alcoholic."

He poured out the story of his childhood living with her drinking and also what had happened that very afternoon.

"All my life I've tried to honor my mother. To be a good son. To be there for her." His chest heaved. "I've struggled to know where my duty to her ends and where her personal responsibility should begin."

Nodding, the pastor leaned forward. "As a boy, I asked myself that many times. It doesn't make the hurt they inflict any less, but addicts are master manipulators at putting the blame for their behaviors elsewhere. Usually on those who love them the most. Instead of owning the disease, they deny the problem. Their stock in trade is guilt and shame to force loved ones to enable their behavior."

Taking in his words, Tanner choked back his emotions.

Pastor Bryant opened his hands. "These were the unspoken rules in the home where I grew up—don't talk, don't trust, don't feel."

Tanner nodded.

"We lived in a conspiracy of silence to never tell anyone what was really going on. There were so many broken promises and forgotten occasions in my family. I never knew what mood I'd find my father in when I came home from school."

The pastor took a breath, then went on. "It was better to never trust anyone. To stop feeling anything at all, so when my father let me down again it wouldn't hurt so much. But one day, after my father punched my mother in the face, I found the courage to tell my teacher. It wasn't easy, but it changed my life for the better."

"How did your mother react?"

The reverend gave him a sad smile. "At first, she was angry with me for not keeping our family's dirty little secret. Yet lying to cover up my father's drinking only prevented him from facing the consequences of his actions. Losing the respect of others and, ultimately, his family.

"What happened with your father?"

Reverend Bryant sighed. "I'd love to tell you he stopped drinking. But he never did. My mom and I built a new life without him. My father died an embittered alcoholic, who drank himself to death at the age of fifty-seven. To the end, he refused to take responsibility for his own decisions or seek help."

It killed Tanner to think of his mother suffering a similar fate.

"Here's what you have to understand, son. You didn't cause this to happen to your mother. You can't control the choices she makes."

Pastor Bryant's kind eyes regarded him. "And hear this if nothing else—you can't cure her. You can't fix her. You can't rescue her. There's only one person who can, and you aren't Him."

Tanner ran his hand over his face. "So what am I supposed to do now, Pastor Bryant?"

"Love her."

Tanner stared at him.

"Love her enough to be honest with her about how her disease has impacted you. Offer your support and make sure she knows she will not be alone. Alcoholism can't be cured, but it can be treated and she can live a healthy, fulfilling life."

Reverend Bryant gripped the arms of his chair. "This is the hardest part—love her enough not to cushion her from the consequences if she refuses treatment. You'll need to set boundaries. And detach with love."

He frowned and dropped his gaze to the floor.

"You and SandraLynn will be in my prayers. I'm available anytime, for any reason. I can also provide you with a network of supportive resources for family members struggling to cope with a loved one's illness."

Over the next few days, he thought a lot about what Reverend Bryant shared. He listened to the podcasts the pastor sent him. One night, he stole away from Truelove to the county seat to attend an Al-Anon meeting for family members of people struggling with addiction.

But there could be no further postponement of the conversation he'd been putting off for years. He waited until he was sure she was sober.

"We need to talk, Mom."

Her eyes narrowed. "Why? So you can preach at me again?"

"I'm not—" He took a breath. With Pastor Bryant's help, he'd written down and practiced what he wanted—needed—to say to his mother.

"I'm concerned by how much you're drinking. You're putting yourself at risk."

She folded her arms across her bathrobe. "I do not have a drinking problem."

"You are a functioning alcoholic. And the drinking is getting worse."

She snorted. "I'm perfectly in control."

"The drinking is in control of *you*."

Her eyes watered. "You don't understand what I've been through."

But Tanner knew he mustn't let her guilt him into excusing her behavior.

"Mom, I don't think you understand how your drinking has hurt me. All my life. Your erratic mood swings. The lack of stability. Me having to parent you instead of the other way around."

"How dare you!" The tears in her eyes dried as quickly as they'd appeared.

"This has to stop, Mom." He took a deep breath. "*I* have to stop."

"What kind of loving son walks away from his mother?" she shouted.

And there it was. Shame.

"I'm the sort of son who loves you too much to lie for you, to cover for you anymore."

He looked at her. "Only you can make the change in yourself. You are not alone. You've never been alone. I'm here for you. But even better, you have a God who loves you devotedly."

"What has God ever done for me?" she shrieked.

Her hair disheveled, her eyes wild, she absolutely broke his heart.

"There is help out there, Mom. You have only to ask." He exhaled. "We could both use some time to cool down. But I'd like to talk again."

Her chin lifted. "As far as I'm concerned, this topic is closed."

Part of him wanted so desperately to take back everything he'd said. To not hold her accountable. To continue to enable her. Because that's what she wanted—for him to give in.

But he couldn't turn a blind eye any longer. Couldn't pretend everything was all right. Nothing was all right.

Turning on his heel, he headed toward the door.

God, please open her eyes to her need of You.

"That's right," she yelled. "Walk away. Just like *he* did."

Tanner froze.

"You're just like him. Just like your father."

The venom in her words smote his heart. He told himself it was the disease talking. Not the lovely, gentle woman who used to tuck him into bed at night and make him chocolate chip–pancake faces in the mornings.

He didn't turn around. "I love you, Mom." In that moment, he'd never loved her more.

She would either get the help she needed. Or she wouldn't. But the burden of her well-being was no longer his to bear.

Then he did the hardest thing he'd ever done.
He walked out the door.

Tanner went straight from his mom's house to Maddie's. She'd tried to warn him about his mom, but he hadn't wanted to see the red flags right under his nose.

One look at his face, and she pulled him into a hug. Sitting in her vanilla-scented kitchen, he told her what had happened.

Tears coursed down his cheeks. Maddie cried with him. At some point, Coach joined them.

Embarrassed at his display of emotion, Tanner swiped his face with his hand. "Sorry to unload on you."

"Don't apologize." Coach shook his head. "Tears cleanse the heart and enable us to heal."

He did feel better. Lighter.

But he didn't think it appropriate to take the Lovetts up on their offer to move into their spare room. Especially not the way he felt for Maddie.

It was Maddie, though, who found him a place. She arranged for him to temporarily bunk with Zach Stone in the apartment above the auto body shop.

Over the next few days, his mom went radio silent. Just as well. He didn't know what else to say to her.

Mr. Jackson had become a friend and mentor. Tanner shared his tentative dream of working with remedial kids after Coach returned to the job.

"To get my license, I'd need to take the usual teacher training classes. And perhaps get counseling certification to help them." He flushed. "Me, a teacher. Crazy, huh?"

"I think you would make an excellent teacher, Tanner." The older gentleman gave him a small smile. "I would be honored to walk you through the application process and provide support as you take the classes you need."

"You'd be willing to do that? For me?"

"In the trenches of making a difference in these young people's lives, you, Tanner Price, are a valued colleague."

At the end of football practice Wednesday, he'd just dismissed the boys from the locker room when Walter received a phone call. Stepping out, the retired judge reappeared a few minutes later with GeorgeAnne at his side.

Tanner sank like a stone onto a bench. "What's happened to my mother, Miss GeorgeAnne?"

She looked as distraught as he'd ever seen her. "There's been a car accident."

He berated himself for not taking her keys when he had the chance. She would have fought him, but he could have alerted the police. It would have meant turning in his own mother, but anything would be better than this wrenching agony.

"Is she dead, Miss GeorgeAnne?" he rasped. Anguish like a heavy boulder crushed his chest.

"No, dear heart." GeorgeAnne sat on one side

of him and Walter sat on the other. "But she is in the ER."

He dreaded to ask, but he had to know. "Did she hurt someone?"

"Only herself." GeorgeAnne cradled his cheek. "And as usual, you."

"SandraLynn crashed into a tree." Walter touched his arm. "Come on, I'll drive you to the hospital."

Tanner looked at GeorgeAnne. "The last time we spoke... Things didn't end well between us."

The compassion in his neighbor's eyes spoke volumes. "I know, but SandraLynn's asking for you."

Bill promised to lock the building. "Is there anything I can do for you, Tanner?"

He, who'd never had a father, found himself suddenly awash with father figures—Coach, Mr. Jackson, Walter and Bill.

"Would you let Maddie know, sir?" He bit his lip to keep it from trembling. "And please ask Pastor Bryant to meet me at the hospital."

On the thirty-minute drive over the mountain to the regional hospital, he had plenty of time to ponder what he would say to his mother.

Leaving GeorgeAnne and Walter in the reception area, he followed the ER nurse through the swinging double doors.

Had it only been two and a half months ago he'd been here with Maddie to see Coach?

Since then, he'd experienced what felt like a lifetime of joy, triumph and happiness.

Now, his stomach cramping, he felt hardly able to breathe. Anxiety strangled his throat.

But the woman he found in the ER cubicle was a shell of the person who only a few days ago had heaped abuse upon his head.

With streaks of dried blood on her shirt and a row of stitches across her forehead, she was a broken woman at rock bottom.

At the sight of him, she burst into racking sobs. No matter what she'd said or done, she was his mother and she always would be.

Going to her, he opened his arms.

"You were right about me," his mother wept on his shoulder. "I am an alcoholic."

Acknowledging the truth was a crucial step.

"Just before the car slammed into the tree, the mess I've made of my life literally flashed before my eyes." She lifted her head. "The sounds of the crunching metal were terrible. I knew I was going to die. Before I blacked out, I begged God to give me another chance to be the mother you deserve." Her voice hitched.

A look of wonder filled her gaze. "And He did. I woke up in the ambulance." Breaking into fresh sobs, she pleaded for his forgiveness after a lifetime of hurt.

"I know I have a long road ahead of me on this journey to sobriety. It won't be easy." She took a breath. "But I'm ready to do whatever it takes to beat this, however long it takes." Her eyes beseeched him. "Just don't give up on me."

"I won't," he promised the woman who'd broken almost every promise she'd ever made to him.

"Please don't stop loving me, son."

He hugged her fiercely. "Never, Mom. Never."

A little while later, he returned to the waiting area. Pastor Bryant had joined GeorgeAnne and Walter.

GeorgeAnne rose. "How is she?"

"The doctor wants to keep her overnight for observation." He released a pent-up breath. "But she's ready to seek treatment for her alcoholism."

GeorgeAnne clasped her hands under her chin. "Praise God."

Walter touched his arm. "The news we've been praying for."

Tanner raked his hand through his hair. "The doctor would prefer she transfer to a residential recovery program right away, if a placement can be found."

Reverend Bryant cleared his throat. "About four hours from Truelove, there's a wonderful, long-term treatment center in the Sandhills. I've referred several people there."

"Do you think they'd have an available spot for my mom tomorrow, though?"

The reverend got out his phone. "Let me make a call."

GeorgeAnne squared her shoulders. "We'll pray that they do."

While they waited, GeorgeAnne commandeered a small section of the reception area.

Pastor Bryant held the phone away from his mouth. "There is an opening if you want it."

"I do."

The reverend put him on the phone with the director. The facility was prepared to receive her upon discharge tomorrow morning. Tanner would need to check her in and complete the paperwork.

"We got your back, Coach." Walter smiled. "Bill and I will work the team extra hard in your absence."

GeorgeAnne put in a call to Judy Moore to arrange for a substitute to cover Tanner's other responsibilities at the school.

He gripped Pastor Bryant's phone. "What about the cost?" he asked the director.

Several things became immediately apparent. The help his mother needed was expensive. And the likelihood of making enough money to afford her treatment outside working the oil rig wasn't feasible. It was a painful, hope-crushing reality check.

Making a verbal commitment to hold the space, he got off the phone. He pinched the bridge of his nose.

"What's wrong?" GeorgeAnne growled.

Staring down the sudden bleakness of his future, he scrubbed his face with his hand.

"After the championship game on Saturday, I'll have to leave Truelove to pay for her treatment."

"No." GeorgeAnne's face crumpled. "I urge you to reconsider. To pray about it."

He shrugged. "From the beginning, you and I

both knew this thing between Maddie and I could only end one way."

GeorgeAnne grabbed his arm. "That girl loves you so much."

"Which is exactly why I have to do this."

He could see no other way forward.

GeorgeAnne shook her head. "You'll break her heart."

Leaving Truelove—leaving Maddie—was already breaking his.

Chapter Fourteen

After receiving Bill's text about SandraLynn, Maddie spent the rest of Wednesday night trying to contact Tanner. But each call went straight to voicemail.

She left message after message assuring him of her prayers. That she was thinking about him. That she was there for him.

Finally, she reached GeorgeAnne. "Is Miss SandraLynn okay? How's Tanner coping?"

"SandraLynn is going to be all right. She's made the decision to enter an alcohol treatment facility. Tanner will take her there tomorrow."

Maddie gasped. "That's wonderful. Tanner must be so thrilled."

"He's... He's tired, Maddie."

There was an odd note in the older woman's voice.

"I'll be at the hospital in thirty minutes, Miss GeorgeAnne."

"Don't come," she barked.

Maddie blinked into the phone.

"It's late." The Double Name Club leader sighed. "So very late."

Not that late. Not even her usual bakery bedtime yet.

"He'll reach out to you when he's able." GeorgeAnne's voice softened. "Pray for him, Maddie."

"Of course, Miss GeorgeAnne. Always."

"I failed him. And you," the older woman rasped.

Her eyes widened. "No, Miss GeorgeAnne. Tanner told me how much you've been there for him and his mother."

She'd never heard the indefatigable matchmaker so subdued.

"You are the dearest woman, Madeline Lovett. I'd long hoped—" Her voice broke off into a sob.

"Miss GeorgeAnne, are you all right?"

"Forgive this old woman, Maddie. I'm so sorry."

She had no clue what GeorgeAnne was talking about. But proper Southern manners being what they were ...

"Of course I forgive you, Miss GeorgeAnne."

"Perhaps it's time I retired and passed the torch to younger, more relevant leadership."

Maddie could no more imagine a Truelove without GeorgeAnne at the helm of the Double Name Club than she could imagine a world without butter.

The next morning, she started on her final special-occasion cake orders. Christmas was only a week away. The state championship was in two days.

All day, she kept expecting to hear from Tanner, but she didn't. She hoped getting his mother checked into the recovery program had gone well for both of them.

That evening, it was with a great deal of anticipation she headed to the Jar. The last team-building night of the season, she knew Tanner wouldn't miss this final opportunity to encourage the team.

For once, her hair cooperated. Her friend Kelsey, the queen of fashion, had helped her pick out the royal blue peacoat. She looked good in that color. Kelsey had told her so.

She was a tad later than usual. From the vehicles parked out front and the activity buzzing beyond the glass-plated windows lining Main Street, the gang was already chowing down.

Clutching the box piled high with her Blond Bombshell Brownies, she walked into the diner.

Tanner waited for her inside the door. Maddie's heart did the usual swoony thing it did whenever she was in the same room with the handsome football coach. "Hey," she breathed.

Her smile matched the exhilaration she felt after not seeing him for twenty-four hours.

She readjusted the box in her arms. "I'll join you at the table for dinner."

"We need to talk, Maddie."

"Absolutely. Let me put this—"

"Can we walk over to the square?"

She raised her brows. "It's freezing outside. After dinner, we could—"

"It has to be now, Maddie." He jabbed his hands in his coat pockets. "Please."

Her gaze flitted around the crowded café. GeorgeAnne, ErmaJean, IdaLee and Glorieta wouldn't meet her gaze.

A cold, hard knot of dread settled in the pit of her stomach.

"Okay..." she whispered.

She followed him in silence across the street beyond the perimeter of trees into the holiday-festooned but deserted square.

He gestured toward the bench. "Let's sit down."

"I think I'd rather stand." Wishing she'd thought to hand off the brownies to someone in the café, she hugged the box to her new coat. "How is your mom?"

He hunched his shoulders. "I believe she's going to succeed this time. She and Pastor Bryant talked the entire way. She's really seeking God, and she's ready to commit to overcoming this disease. The facility is a phenomenal place."

"That's wonderful, Tanner." She'd been half afraid that after what happened, he would shut down again. "It's everything I've been praying for your mom."

He shuffled his feet. "The price tag for her wellness is hefty. After the final game Saturday, I'll be leaving Truelove and returning to the oil rig job." For the first time, he looked at her directly. "The job I postponed for the sake of the team."

It was not what she'd expected to hear. She set the box down with a thunk onto the bench.

Her lips parted. "What about us, Tanner?"

"There can be no us, Maddie. One day, you'll see I did you a favor."

"Please don't do this." Her breath hitched. "There has to be another way."

"There is no other way."

After the breakthroughs he'd made, he was reverting to form. But she wasn't her father's daughter for nothing.

She took hold of his hand. He flinched, but she didn't let go. "You love me, Tanner. For once, allow yourself to feel. Feel how much you love me."

He pulled his hand from hers. "Love is not the issue."

"Love is the only issue that matters." She threw out her hands. "You've proven what an outside-the-box thinker you are. It's why you succeed. It's part of what makes you so special. We'll find a way to make this work for your mom. You don't have to fight this battle alone."

"This is not your problem, Maddie."

"Don't shut me out." She lifted her chin. "Say it, Tanner. Say it just once. For your sake, if not for mine. Tell me you love me."

He crossed his arms over his coat. "Forgive me for hurting you, Maddie." His breath fogged in the winter chill. "I've got to do whatever it takes to give my mother this chance."

"Not at the expense of your own happiness. If

you won't say it, then I will." Her gaze locked on his. "I love you, Tanner. You don't have to go to the North Sea alone."

Something flickered in his eyes... Her heart swelled with hope.

In that moment, if he had asked her to give up Truelove, to walk away from Madeline's, her friends and, yes, her family, too—she would have ditched them all.

For a life with him, she would have followed him anywhere in the world. Wherever the job took him.

But he didn't ask.

"It's over for us, Maddie."

The pain in her heart was so swift, sharp and sudden, she feared her knees would buckle. She recognized the stubborn look in his eyes—those beautiful, breaking-her-heart eyes of his.

He'd made up his mind. He'd convinced himself he was doing this for her sake.

From somewhere, she dredged up just enough pride to prevent herself from begging him to reconsider.

She bit off the sob rising in her throat. She couldn't—wouldn't—cry. She still had that much Lovett dignity left.

Last night, GeorgeAnne had known... A lot of pieces of the last confusing twenty-four hours suddenly fell into place.

She picked up the box and thrust it at him. "The boys are looking forward to this, but I'm sure you'll understand why I don't feel up to delivering it myself."

A small breeze blew a curl across her cheek. He reached out his hand but stopped just shy of touching her. The sadness on his face made her heart ache.

Tanner dropped his hand. "Be happy," he whispered.

She shook her head. "How can I be without you?" Then she turned and walked away from him.

There would be no happily-ever-after for her without Tanner.

Saturday night found Tanner prowling the sideline in Raleigh at North Carolina State University's Carter-Finley Stadium.

It had been a long, three-hour bus ride from Truelove. And a long journey to the state championship. Not only in terms of mileage.

The Bobcats were number one in their division with a record of 14–1. Only one team stood between Truelove and the state title. But the boys faced the Triad team with the most state champion wins in North Carolina sports history.

Earlier in the locker room, he reminded the guys tonight was the culmination of a lot of hard work. Hopes and dreams would either be fulfilled or dashed. There could be no more playing it safe. No more hedging their bets. It was time to lay it all on the line. To leave everything they had on the field.

Tanner told them how proud he was. How proud

Coach was. He told them to do their best. Not only in the game but with the rest of their lives.

He thanked them for allowing him the honor of walking the road to the championship with them.

Then he sent them out to the field to win one more time—not for their families or him or Truelove. But to win it for themselves.

Waiting for Kyle to kick off the game, he couldn't resist turning toward the stands where he saw the Truelove fans huddled together.

He spotted so many people who'd made the long journey with him over the football season. So many friends—the Brendans, the Atkinsons, the McKendrys, the Crenshaws.

Tanner was grateful. So grateful.

Yet he continued to search for the one face most dear to him. The one who'd been by his side every step of the way cheering the team and him onward to victory.

After what happened in the square, the last two days had been excruciating. With his mom in rehab, the house had been as silent as the tomb of his heart. He'd had far too much time to think. And to grieve what he'd thrown away.

Only now could he admit it to himself. He loved Maddie Lovett. Deeply. Irrevocably.

He suspected some part of him had always loved her.

It had taken everything within him to not respond to her plea to take her with him.

But he couldn't stay in Truelove, and he loved Maddie Lovett too much to ask her to leave.

His head told him this was for the best. His heart shuddered from the loss of her. For what a future without her would mean.

Finally, halfway up the stadium bleachers, he found her, with GeorgeAnne and ErmaJean on either side of her.

She'd promised him she'd be there for him as he coached her father's team toward this moment. And here she was—despite how he'd broken her heart.

Maddie always kept her promises to him.

It was a huge arena, but he knew the second her gaze fastened on his. He saw his own emotions reflected in her eyes.

Love. Regret. And sadness. Such sadness.

His heart was heavy, but she would be all right. Her support network in Truelove was vast. She had her dad and her friends. She had Madeline's.

As much as it hurt him to contemplate it, one day she would fall in love again.

But with a certainty deep in his gut, he knew he would not. There would never be anyone for him but her.

Yet he loved her enough to want for her all she deserved. A husband. Children. A home of her own.

The whistle blew. He focused on the field. He could give her nothing, except maybe this.

A state championship for Truelove.

The game got underway. The teams were well-matched. Truelove would score a touchdown and extra point only to have the opposing team do the same.

Back and forth across the scrimmage lines, the battle raged. Two worthy teams, but only one could lay claim ultimately to the greatest prize of high school football—state champions.

In the fourth quarter the make or break moment came. When the other team's punt was downed at Truelove's forty-yard line with 2:20 left on the clock, the Bobcats took over.

On a third-and-fourth at Truelove's twenty-yard line, his golden arm quarterback, Randall, found Javier, the fastest wide receiver in the conference, for a twenty-yard touchdown pass down the middle.

Like icing on the cake, Kyle's field goal was good. The scoreboard read Bobcats 56; Grizzlies 47.

With thirty seconds left in the fourth quarter, Tanner and the team ran out the clock. At the final buzzer, the guys on the field froze. For a second, a hush fell over the spectators. The Triad team appeared stunned. Disbelief shone from the faces of the Truelove team—his team.

They looked at him.

A rush of joy broke free in his chest. They'd done it. Fist-pumping the air, he, who never showed his emotions, came a few feet off the ground and roared.

The Truelove crowd went wild. The players, on

the field and on the bench, rushed him. Hurley, Kyle, Randall, DaShonte and Javier.

Every single one. Dear to his heart. His boys. His team. His guys.

Crying. Laughing. Slapping each other on the back. Sometimes all three at once. They lifted him on their shoulders and carried him out to the middle of the field.

Nine years ago, he'd been here. A state champion in his own right. But this time...this time was sweeter.

Later during the trophy ceremony, he caught a final glimpse of Maddie in the stands. Despite the tears of joy coursing across her cheeks, her face was wreathed in a smile just for him.

Thank you, she mouthed.

He should be thanking her for pushing him into accepting the temporary coaching position. Leading to one of the greatest moments of his life.

The official spoke into the microphone. By the time he glanced over again to the stands, she was gone.

After the awards were handed out, Tanner left the stadium with the team. They would return to Truelove in the morning. But for tonight, after a great deal of fundraising, the Booster Club had secured hotel rooms for the players and their families.

Some of the boys had never stayed in a hotel before. Yet another demonstration of how Truelove cared for their own.

One of the ballrooms had been reserved for a

late after-game celebration. Everyone who'd made the trek from Truelove to Raleigh was invited. The players, their families, the fans mixed and mingled. Lots of laughter. Lots of food.

"None as good as Miss Kara's," Hurley declared.

"Not even close to Madeline's quality," DaShonte scoffed.

Without a backward glance, the boys boycotted the dessert bar. Their loyalty would have brought tears to her eyes.

He'd done what he set out to do. Mission accomplished. But despite his happiness at their well-deserved win, a hollowness gnawed at him.

Everything was so mixed up in his head and in his heart. He missed Maddie so bad, his insides ached.

Never one for victory laps, he wandered into the marble-floored lobby to head to his room.

"Coach Price!" Principal Moore flagged him down. "Might I have a word?" Beside her stood Maddie's father.

"Coach, what're you doing here?"

Maddie's father slapped him on the back. "Where else would I be but watching my protégé lead the team to the championship?"

"I didn't see you in the stands."

"Didn't watch from the stands." Coach grinned. "Back when dinosaurs roamed the earth, I played a little football in Carter-Finley myself."

He'd forgotten Coach had been part of the Wolfpack Nation.

Coach winked at him. "I know a few guys. Pulled a few strings. Watched the game from the VIP suite."

Maddie's father pulled him into a hug. "I can't tell you how proud I am of how you've led the team, Tanner."

"*Your* team, Coach." Tanner jutted his chin. "Your championship."

"No, son. They are your guys. Your win. It's your job if you want it."

Tanner gaped at him. "What are you saying, Coach?"

"I've decided to retire."

"But—"

"Hear me out." Coach held up his hand. "It's been a good run. But in light of my recent health scare, I've reevaluated my priorities. There's other paths I want to explore." He squeezed Judy Moore's arm. "Other dreams I want to pursue."

"Does Maddie know you're retiring?"

"I shared my news with her yesterday. She's happy for me and Judy."

Principal Moore faced Tanner. "Based on Don's recommendation, mine and senior faculty member Lucian Jackson, the school board would like to offer you the full-time coaching position."

"I never expected anything like this," he sputtered. "I'd love to accept, but—"

"If you're interested in getting your North Carolina teaching license, we're willing to work with you for however long it takes to make it happen."

Tanner stared at them. "Teaching and coaching? I'd love nothing more, but my mom..."

His disappointment sharp, he looked away.

"Did I also mention the school athletic director receives a very healthy salary?"

His gaze snapped to Principal Moore.

"I think you'll find it quite sufficient for your mother's recovery program."

GeorgeAnne and Walter stepped out of the shadows.

The distinguished former judge put his hand on Tanner's shoulder. "And if it doesn't, you have many friends willing to stand in the gap with you. Trust us, son. We'll work through any shortfall together."

He couldn't believe this was truly happening.

"Thank you, sir." He shook Coach's hand. "Thank you, ma'am." He threw his arms around a startled Principal Moore.

He could stay in Truelove. He had the opportunity to live a life of purpose. To make a difference. A chance to leverage his life and build his own legacy of service to others.

Thank You, God.

Everything he'd ever longed for, except for one thing.

The home he'd always wanted with the one person who'd believed in him from the beginning.

His heart jack-knifed. In pushing Maddie away, he'd made the biggest mistake of his life.

When his mom relapsed, he'd let faith lapse, too.

But faith was only as good as the object in which it is placed. He should have trusted God instead of relying on his own, very fallible understanding.

Could he convince Maddie to give him another chance? Was it too late?

He turned to Coach. "I'd like to ask your forgiveness for hurting your daughter, sir. It's always been hard for me to be open about my feelings."

"What are your feelings for Maddie?"

"I love her. I'd like your blessing in asking Maddie to marry me." He locked eyes with her father. "Without that, I won't take this any further with Maddie."

Coach folded his arms across his chest. "How do I know three months from now, you won't hurt her again?"

"I think the past few months demonstrates I am a man who keeps his promises, Coach." He squared his shoulders. "I promise you in front of all these witnesses, I'll spend the rest of my life loving her and making sure you never regret placing your daughter's hand in mine."

Everyone stilled. His heart pounded. For a long, uncomfortable moment Coach examined him. As was her father's right.

If God ever blessed him with a daughter, he'd do the same.

Tanner held his breath as Coach raked him from head to toe with those keenly penetrating, all-seeing eyes of his. Drilling down to the core of his character.

Please, Lord...

"You've always felt like a son to me, Tanner." Coach pulled him into a bear hug. "I think it's high time we make it official, don't you?"

The relief was so profound, he sagged. Walter gave him a broad wink. Judy Moore smiled at him.

If he didn't know better—GeorgeAnne wasn't exactly warm and fuzzy—he thought he saw the Double Name Club matriarch wipe a tear from her cheek.

Coach thumped him on the back. "Real question is, how do you plan to make this right with my girl?"

Seized with a sudden idea, he angled to GeorgeAnne. "I can hardly believe I'm saying this, but I need the matchmakers' help."

The older woman pursed her thin lips. "What are you thinking?"

He sketched out the plan taking shape in his head.

"Never fear, dear heart." GeorgeAnne pushed her glasses higher on the bridge of her nose. "The Double Name Club is on it."

Like he'd told the team before the game, he had a lot of hard work ahead of him. In the next few days, his hopes and dreams would either be fulfilled or dashed.

There could be no more playing it safe. No more hedging his bets. It was time to lay it all on the line.

He didn't fool himself. The stakes were high.

There'd be obstacles to overcome. But he resolved to leave everything he had on the field.

To win the greatest prize of all—her heart.

Chapter Fifteen

Unable to face anyone at the after-party, Maddie drove back to Truelove by herself. She cried all the way home, finally collapsing into bed in the wee hours of the morning.

Sunday wasn't one of her better days. She decided not to join the congratulatory well-wishers scheduled to meet the returning bus that afternoon at the square.

With SandraLynn in the residential recovery program, there was nothing and no one to keep Tanner in Truelove. Maddie couldn't cope with watching him leave town again. This time forever.

She spent a miserable day devouring a carton of peppermint-chocolate ice cream. Even the thought of baking failed to cheer her up.

And the day Maddie Lovett didn't want to bake was a sad day indeed.

She'd expected her dad to return from Raleigh for the parade, but by Sunday evening, he remained a no-show.

Perhaps it was better if she didn't talk to him

until tomorrow. Maybe by then, she could manage to stop crying.

She lay in bed a long time, torturing herself with memories of the last two and a half months with Tanner. Reliving every look, every smile. Trying in vain to wrap her mind around the fact that the future she'd dreamed of with him was never meant to be.

Eventually, she cried herself to sleep. Around midnight, she heard her father come home, but emotionally spent, she soon fell asleep again.

When her alarm went off at 5:00 a.m., for the first time in the history of Madeline's, she rolled over and buried her head under the pillow.

A little while later, her dad tapped on her bedroom door. "Don't you have to get to the bakery, Maddie girl?"

Ughhhhhh... Why couldn't people leave her alone? But the conscientious part of her wouldn't let her rest until she got out of bed.

Glaring at her bleary-eyed appearance in the mirror, she swiped a hank of unruly hair out of her face. No reason to put on lip gloss. And there was certainly no one to put on hair product for.

This was her new life. She was going to have to get used to the reality that Tanner was gone—for good.

When she emerged, her father was nowhere to be found. At Madeline's, with Preston out of school for the holidays, she had him and Ann to man the front.

Hiding in the back, she threw herself into a frenzy of baking.

It felt like everyone in Truelove had decided to bring home one last sweet treat before she closed for the holidays. That afternoon, Ann left early. Chloe's mom had to help her daughter prepare for some big shindig tomorrow night.

Heartsick and weary, Maddie was turning the sign on the door to Closed when Preston handed her a white sheet torn from the order pad.

"Last minute cake." He smiled. "I got the details like you showed me."

Two days before Christmas Eve, someone had called in a last-minute cake order?

Maddie scanned the order. A large Christmas cake. Enough to feed a hundred people.

"The client was insistent about the filling, icing and decorations. I drew it out for you."

Her eyes widened at the intricate design sketched on the back of the paper.

Preston put on his jacket. "Oh, and they said the cake will need to be ready by five p.m. Christmas Eve."

Her gaze darted to her youngest part-time employee. This is the result of hiding all day. If she'd answered the phone, she would've politely refused an order like this so close to Christmas.

Preston was such a hard worker. She didn't have the heart to tell him the deadline for special-occasion cakes was long past.

Besides, it wasn't like she had anything better to do.

"I hope you have the most wonderful Christmas ever, Miss Maddie."

Not likely, but she wished him a Merry Christmas, too.

After he left, she realized she should have asked him about the delivery. There was only one clue written in his tightly scrawled teenage handwriting.

Delivery instructions to follow.

One of those clients. Great. Hopefully, the client would be in touch soon.

At home, she found a note from her dad. He and Judy would be away this evening, making last-minute Christmas preparations.

What preparations? Since her mother died, Maddie had done all the shopping, wrapping, decorating and cooking for every single holiday.

Sick and tired of being sick and tired, she had to do something to cheer up. She loved Christmas. And she wasn't going to let Tanner Price ruin it for her.

Maddie texted Kara, hoping for a visit with baby Noèle. But citing the baby's nap schedule, her dear friend begged off until another time.

She reached out to Chloe. Available for coffee and a chat?

But Chloe turned her down. Busier than I expected. Raincheck after Christmas?

Oh, yeah. There'd been that thing happening with Chloe's mom.

It was the same story with Gemma, Kelsey and Mollie. Everyone was busy. The promise of cupcakes even failed to lure Zach over.

She spent the evening alone.

Once again, she fell asleep waiting for her dad to return. When she got up the next morning, she found he'd come home and gone out again.

She hadn't seen her father since the game Saturday. If she didn't know better, she'd think he was avoiding her.

Feeling blue, she started on the last-minute Christmas cake.

Her friends knew how she felt about Tanner. But no one reached out to check on her. No one called. No one stopped by to inquire after her welfare.

Maybe it wasn't so bad she had a baking project to keep her busy. With Madeline's closed for the holidays, she spent the entire day baking cake layers, frosting the layers and embellishing the cake within an inch of its life.

Still no address for delivery. By two o'clock, she was starting to panic. But then she remembered special-occasion cakes required a deposit.

When he took the order, Preston would have run a credit card through. She was contemplating returning to the store to check the credit card slip when her father strolled into the house.

Standing at the sink cleaning her decorating tools, she dried her hands on a towel. "Hello, stranger."

"A real work of art, honey pie." He admired the

cake on the counter. "I'm sure everyone will enjoy it tonight."

"You know who ordered it? You know where I'm supposed to deliver it?"

"'Course I do." He stuck his finger in the bowl of leftover icing.

She slapped at his hand. "Care to share?"

He gave the bowl a pointed look. "Do you?"

She pushed the bowl at him. "The only info Preston received was that someone would provide delivery instructions."

He coated his index finger in icing. "That would be me."

She took the bowl out of his hands.

"Hey," he protested.

"Details, Dad."

He shrugged. "Judy hired a new coach. The event tonight at the high school is to officially welcome him into the Truelove fold. I'll be passing the proverbial football over to him." He stuck his finger in his mouth.

"A new coach? So soon?" She gaped at him. "Why is this the first I'm hearing about it?"

Her dad's gaze slid away. "When Judy found the right candidate, she had to act quickly. The whole thing came together sort of suddenly."

She frowned. "You called in the cake order?"

"Not me." His gaze cut to hers. "You'll be my escort, won't you?"

"After what's happened with Tanner..." She bit her lip. "I don't think I can go, Dad."

Her father put his arm around her. "Going will make you feel better."

She shook her head.

"I don't ask much of you, sugar girl—"

She removed herself from his arm. "Seriously?"

"It's important. A huge milestone. I can't do this without you." He sighed. "Please come, Maddie."

Her father had been the high school football coach her entire life. He was excited about his new future, but tonight was likely to be bittersweet for him. It was the end of an era.

Maddie's dad leaned against the counter. "You have to deliver the cake anyway."

"Or you could take it for me."

He gave her such a hangdog look, she laughed.

"Nice try, Dad, but there's no way I can get ready in time."

Sensing capitulation, his face transformed. "You've got plenty of time to get dolled up."

Maddie tugged at one of her long curls. "Have you ever met my hair, Dad?"

"Get going then." He gave her a small push. "Oh, and Maddie?"

She surrendered to the inevitable. "Yes, Dad?"

"Your hair is only slightly less beautiful than your heart."

The next few hours were a whirlwind. Her father insisted she put on the emerald-green crushed-velvet dress in the back of her closet she'd actually never had the occasion to wear. She paired it with black tights and boots, and donned her long crimson wool coat and a winter-white scarf to complete her outfit.

She was beyond surprised to find her father—a man who preferred athletic wear above all else—dressed in a suit and red tie.

In contrast to the usual laidback mountain life, this celebration promised to be the social event of the Truelove Christmas season.

"Looking good, Dad."

Peering out the window at the sky, he straightened and smiled. "Don't want to embarrass you in front of the home crowd."

"You look dapper in your suit." She adjusted his tie. "I think Judy will approve."

He insisted on driving. She was a nervous wreck until they arrived—cake unscathed—at the school.

"Whew!" He wiped his brow. "I've had less nail-biting playoffs than getting that cake here tonight."

She glanced around the overflowing parking lot. "Are we late?"

"Not a bit." Carrying the cake box, he herded her toward the field. "Just in time."

They must be late if everyone was already seated in the bleachers.

Outside the shuttered concession stand, Ann appeared in her Sunday best. "I'll take it from here."

What on earth?

"We're supposed to enter when they call my name." Her father hustled her behind the bleachers to the end of the field. "Don't want to miss our cue."

"Ladies and gentlemen," the announcer's microphone crackled. "Join me in welcoming Truelove's very own Coach Donald Lovett."

"Cutting it kind of close, Dad," she murmured.

They stepped onto the field. On either side of the goal post, the football team had formed two lines. Taking her father's arm, they walked between them into the blazing lights. The guys grinned at her.

Randall. Javier. DaShonte. Tender-hearted Hurley was trying not to cry. Kyle.

But the line stretched far longer than just the current players. Sam Gibson. Clay McKendry. Luke Morgan. And so many more.

Past and present teams—all her father's boys—had come to honor him.

Her vision went blurry.

"None of that, now." Her father patted her hand in the crook of his arm. "This is going to be the happiest of nights."

She was so glad Judy was giving him this moment of recognition, especially after missing the season.

This was why she loved Truelove. Why she never wanted to live anywhere else.

When they joined Judy center field, the players filed off to find seats in the stands. Her father's lady love did a brief rundown on his illustrious career at Truelove. Then Judy presented her dad with a lifetime achievement plaque.

With the field lights blazing, it was hard for Maddie to pick out individuals, but the stands appeared packed with Truelove citizens.

Her father spoke a few words about what a privilege it had been to coach at Truelove High. How dear each young man was to him.

"And finally, I want to say a special thanks to my beloved daughter, Maddie. Her support has been the bedrock of my life. She's the real heart of any success I've achieved."

"Oh, Dad," she whispered.

Stepping away from the mic, he handed the plaque to Judy. Taking Maddie's face between his roughened palms, he kissed her forehead. "I love you, Maddie."

"I love you, too, Dad."

Judy returned to the mic. "If you would join me now in giving a real Bobcat welcome to Truelove High's new football coach…"

On the far end, someone walked out of the darkness onto the field under the goalpost.

Judy flashed a smile at Maddie. "…Our very own Tanner Price."

The applause was thunderous.

Her gaze cut between her father and Judy. What was happening here?

As the figure drew closer, she realized it was Tanner. But he stopped on the thirty-yard line.

She gripped her father's sleeve. "I don't understand. He's supposed to be headed to the North Sea."

Her dad smiled at her. "Tanner always wanted to stay, so we found a way to make sure he could."

Maddie's breath caught. "You gave up your job for him."

"I gave up my job for you." Under the lights, tears glistened in her father's eyes. "Be happy, Maddie girl."

Taking Judy's arm, he headed toward Tanner. They shook hands and then embraced. He and Judy walked off toward the sideline.

For a second, standing alone in the middle of the football field, she stared after them. But then Tanner started toward her.

Was this what she thought it was? What she'd hoped and prayed for? Was Tanner going to propose?

Trembling, she watched him cross the twenty-yard distance separating them. He had on a tux. *Wow, he cleans up good.*

"Hey, Maddie," he rasped.

She touched a curl that escaped her beret and dangled below her ear. His gaze followed the movement of her hand before returning to her face.

When he looked at her like that with his heart in his eyes... She put her hand to her throat.

Those eyes of his—no longer inscrutable—it was like looking into the deeply layered depths of a moss-dappled brook.

"I hope you don't mind an audience." He jerked his chin toward the stands. "You've spent so much of your life here supporting others. It seemed appropriate this time they support you. I want the whole town to know how I feel about you."

He removed a box from his pocket and went down on one knee. "I love you, Maddie Lovett."

Tears welling in her eyes, she put her hand to her mouth.

"I love you so much." He opened the box to reveal the most beautiful ring she had ever seen. "Would you do me the honor of becoming my wife? Would you marry me and share my joys and my struggles for the rest of my life?"

"Yes," she whispered. "I will."

"She said yes!" he shouted and slipped the ring on her finger.

The crowd in the bleachers broke into cheers. The Bobcat fight song rang out.

"Seriously?" She laughed. "The band is here, too?"

As the marching band descended onto the field with trumpets blaring, Tanner rose and lifted her off her feet.

He carried her off the field toward the goal post.

She hung on to her beret. "Where are we going?"

"The party's just getting started, Mads." He nuzzled her neck. His cheek felt cold against her neck. "But this time, I'd prefer to kiss you without the whole town watching."

She'd believed the evening couldn't get any more perfect.

Until, just as his lips found hers, tiny snowflakes fell from the dark night sky.

Their engagement party took place in the school gym. The Double Name Club, the ROMEOs and their friends had gone all out to make this the happiest of events for him and Maddie.

At the door, Preston and Hurley took their coats. Under Kelsey's supervision, the utilitarian gymnasium had been transformed into a festive Christmas wonderland. Kara had outdone herself with the food.

Everyone wanted to extend their heartfelt well-wishes for a long and happy life together.

Being Maddie, she had to take a second to love on Baby Noèle. Chloe's Lili ran over to give Maddie a hug, too.

Maddie gazed round the circle of her dearest friends. "You ladies really had me feeling sorry for myself."

Kara laughed. "We've been preoccupied putting this evening together for you and Tanner."

"My father, too?"

"Coach Lovett has been so excited." Chloe rolled her eyes. "Girl, keeping that man from spilling the beans took the combined efforts of the entire town."

"People say I've got a lot of energy?" Kelsey blew out a breath. "Your father is exhausting."

Drawing her away, Tanner brought Maddie to the cake table.

Her mouth dropped. "It was you who called in the order?"

"I did."

She shook her head. "You had me make my own engagement cake?"

"Well, yeah." He grinned. "Who else? You make

the best cakes in the world. Have I told you lately how much I love you?"

She smiled. "Not in the last five minutes."

His mouth brushed the curl dangling at her ear. "I love you forever and always, Maddie Lovett."

She fluttered her lashes at him. "How would you feel about a spring wedding?"

"Won't be football season. I can work with that." He cocked his head. "If a Valentine's wedding isn't an option."

Rising on her tiptoes, she kissed his cheek. "I'll see what Kelsey and I can arrange."

The women wanted Maddie to show off her ring. He left her to it and mingled with coworkers, players and students.

Antisocial as he was, he would have never predicted that. She must be rubbing off on him. But he was among friends.

Maddie had rejoined him when GeorgeAnne stalked over. He'd never seen his neighbor in anything other than jeans and boots.

Was the no-nonsense older woman actually wearing high heels?

"Miss GeorgeAnne, there's one thing I've been wondering..." Maddie bit her lip. "Why did you never try to match me with anyone?"

"You were never forgotten, dear heart." GeorgeAnne threw her a fond look. "The matchmakers had to play a long game for both you and your father. We had to wait for God to bring Tanner home to Himself and to you."

The older woman patted his arm. "I'm sorry SandraLynn couldn't be here tonight to celebrate with you."

"She's where she needs to be for now." Tanner nodded. "I called her this morning. She was thrilled at the news and reminded me she'd always liked Coach's sweet little daughter. So do I."

Maddie squeezed his hand.

Tanner kissed GeorgeAnne's wrinkled cheek. "Thank you for also rallying the troops for my students."

Everyone in Truelove had decided to invest in the kids no one else cared about. Just like Maddie told him, the town cared for its own. And now he'd be there to ensure every kid who passed through his classroom knew he believed in them, too.

As long as he remained in school and kept free of drugs, Hudson would work part-time at Colton's construction company. Brian Allen had hired Leah to work at the hardware store after school.

From the gleam in GeorgeAnne's eyes, he'd need to add the girl to his prayer list. Or was it the other way around? Leah King was a hard nut.

The Double Name Club leader might have finally met her match.

GeorgeAnne waved her bony hand. "It became apparent to the Double Name Club we hadn't devoted enough of our talents to Truelove's educational institutions."

He put his arm around his bride-to-be. "What's

this I hear about the matchmakers retiring, Miss GeorgeAnne?"

"Never." His neighbor scowled. "You should know better than to listen to rumors."

Then her attention was diverted by the group of students clustered around the punch bowl.

Her glacier-blue eyes went frosty. "You, there, young man!" She wagged her finger. "Don't think I didn't see what you did, young lady!"

Off she went to harangue the next generation of future matchmaker mayhem.

As long as there was a Truelove, there would be special people like the matchmakers to ensure love awaited everyone with the courage to embrace it.

Which was, and is, exactly as it should always be.

* * * * *

Dear Reader,

Like the river that bends around the small town of Truelove, several themes have run through the entirety of the series. One has been that in Truelove, neighbors help neighbors. But who is my neighbor? The matchmakers have reminded me that my neighbors aren't just my friends or the people who look, think or act like me. Over the years, in writing about this small patchwork kingdom in the foothills of the Blue Ridge, I've been challenged to act in obedience to the realization that my neighbors are also the easily overlooked, the forgotten, the difficult, the inconvenient people God sometime places in our paths.

I hope you found encouragement in Tanner's faith journey. As he discovers, faith is only as good as the object which it is placed in. Where have you placed your faith? If you have placed your faith in the true hero of your story and mine, you will never be disappointed. I pray this book—this series—has been as much a blessing to you as you have been to me.

Thank you for sharing Maddie's and Tanner's journey with me. It is through Christ, we find our forever Home—the happily-ever-after for which we were created. Thank you for telling your friends how much you enjoy the Truelove matchmaker series.

I'd love to connect with you. You can contact

me at lisa@lisacarterauthor.com or visit lisacarterauthor.com, where you can also subscribe to my author newsletter for news about upcoming book releases and sales.

In His Love,
Lisa Carter

Get up to 4 Free Books!

We'll send you 2 free books from each series you try PLUS a free Mystery Gift.

FREE Value Over **$25**

Both the **Love Inspired®** and **Love Inspired® Suspense** series feature compelling novels filled with inspirational romance, faith, forgiveness and hope.

YES! Please send me 2 FREE novels from the Love Inspired or Love Inspired Suspense series and my FREE gift (gift is worth about $10 retail). After receiving them, if I don't wish to receive any more books, I can return the shipping statement marked "cancel." If I don't cancel, I will receive 6 brand-new Love Inspired Larger-Print books or Love Inspired Suspense Larger-Print books every month and be billed just $7.19 each in the U.S. or $7.99 each in Canada. That is a savings of 20% off the cover price. It's quite a bargain! Shipping and handling is just 50¢ per book in the U.S. and $1.25 per book in Canada.* I understand that accepting the 2 free books and gift places me under no obligation to buy anything. I can always return a shipment and cancel at any time by calling the number below. The free books and gift are mine to keep no matter what I decide.

Choose one:
- ☐ **Love Inspired Larger-Print** (122/322 BPA G36Y)
- ☐ **Love Inspired Suspense Larger-Print** (107/307 BPA G36Y)
- ☐ **Or Try Both!** (122/322 & 107/307 BPA G36Z)

Name (please print)

Address   Apt. #

City   State/Province   Zip/Postal Code

Email: Please check this box ☐ if you would like to receive newsletters and promotional emails from Harlequin Enterprises ULC and its affiliates. You can unsubscribe anytime.

Mail to the Harlequin Reader Service:
IN U.S.A.: P.O. Box 1341, Buffalo, NY 14240-8531
IN CANADA: P.O. Box 603, Fort Erie, Ontario L2A 5X3

Want to explore our other series or interested in ebooks? **Visit www.ReaderService.com or call 1-800-873-8635.**

---

*Terms and prices subject to change without notice. Prices do not include sales taxes, which will be charged (if applicable) based on your state or country of residence. Canadian residents will be charged applicable taxes. Offer not valid in Quebec. This offer is limited to one order per household. Books received may not be as shown. Not valid for current subscribers to the Love Inspired or Love Inspired Suspense series. All orders subject to approval. Credit or debit balances in a customer's account(s) may be offset by any other outstanding balance owed by or to the customer. Please allow 4 to 6 weeks for delivery. Offer available while quantities last.

Your Privacy—Your information is being collected by Harlequin Enterprises ULC, operating as Harlequin Reader Service. For a complete summary of the information we collect, how we use this information and to whom it is disclosed, please visit our privacy notice located at https://corporate.harlequin.com/privacy-notice. Notice to California Residents – Under California law, you have specific rights to control and access your data. For more information on these rights and how to exercise them, visit https://corporate.harlequin.com/california-privacy. For additional information for residents of other U.S. states that provide their residents with certain rights with respect to personal data, visit https://corporate.harlequin.com/other-state-residents-privacy-rights/.

LIRLIS25